LT   Cross, Amanda

Cr   No word from
         Winifred

DATE DUE

NO WORD
FROM
WINIFRED

Also by Amanda Cross
in Thorndike Large Print

DEATH IN A TENURED POSITION

THE THEBAN MYSTERIES

POETIC JUSTICE

THE JAMES JOYCE MURDER

IN THE LAST ANALYSIS

No Word From Winifred

Amanda Cross

THORNDIKE PRESS · THORNDIKE, MAINE

Library of Congress Cataloging in Publication Data:

Cross, Amanda, 1926-
  No word from Winifred.

  Reprint. Originally published: New York : Dutton, c1986.
  1. Large type books. I. Title.
  [PS3558.E4526N6 1986]   813'.54   86-14465
  ISBN 0-89621-740-X (alk. paper)

Large Print edition available in North America by arrangement with E. P. Dutton.

Large Print edition available in the British Commonwealth
by arrangement with Virago Press.

Cover design by James B. Murray.

To Tom F. Driver
For old and new times' sake

One

Laurence R. Fansler, the oldest partner of Darwin Darwin Erasmus and Mendel, was chatting with the next oldest partner in the firm. "Chatting" would have been Fansler's own description of what he was doing, but the word was, in fact, inaccurate. Fansler never chatted. He either commanded or pontificated, and when these modes appeared inappropriate, he attempted a certain tone of bonhomie for which, had he but known it, he was notorious throughout the firm. It meant Fansler wanted something.

In this case, what he wanted was consolation disguised as advice. Toby Van Dine served in all but his place on the stationery as the senior partner of the firm, the Solomon, the father confessor, the mediator, the consoler. He was a quiet man, quietly brilliant, who, unlike his senior, represented the more liberal views characteristic of his generation of lawyers. He had noted, with a certain sadness, that those who made partner these days — after eight or nine arduous years — were singly devoted to selfish interests and their own advancement. He tried not to brood about this, not even to think of it often. But occasionally, the cases the firm had fought in the old days returned to him, pristine in their principled glory. The effects of old age, no doubt. Toby Van Dine had just turned sixty, and was afraid.

"You know these parties we always give," Fansler was muttering. "Started years ago, and became a tradition. One can't stop, that's the trouble." Toby nodded. The Fansler parties, given annually in the fall for the associates, had long since become one of the burdens of the legal life at Dar and Dar, as it was known among lawyers. First- and second-year associates were asked, together with any young professionals in other pursuits whom Fansler's wife Janice could corral. The original idea had been Janice's, or so Fansler claimed, and had been designed to make the young "men" feel more at home in New York, and meet people their own age. Fansler had accommodated, grumbling, to the women lawyers who had to be asked, as well as some of the "dates" brought by his very own associates. There was the year one of the young men had come with his fianceé — if there was another way to describe her, Fansler had no desire to hear it — who was a doctor, and who, on being asked, described the process of getting a catheter into the heart through the femoral artery in detail sufficiently fine and labored to ruin everyone's appetite. But all this was in the past, and could hardly, Toby thought, be Fansler's problem.

"Janice thinks we should ask my sister," Fansler said with a groan.

"But you always ask her," Toby said, "and she never comes."

"I know, I know, but this year the thought is that we should ask her husband — Amhearst, you know. He's teaching at Columbia Law School, and the other partners don't see why we shouldn't cultivate someone on the faculty there, particularly if he's a relative. Janice agrees, of course."

Laurence Fansler had, along with so much else in a rapidly changing world, accepted the fact that his nephews, and even one or two of his nieces, were now lawyers or doctors or working for Goldman Sachs, and had to be asked to his party. But to ask his sister seemed, to Fansler's jaundiced eye, as though Caesar had asked Brutus to brunch.

"I think you're exaggerating, Larry," Toby said. "Kate and Reed aren't that bad. The worst you can probably say for them is that they voted for Mondale and Ferraro in 1984."

"Exactly," Fansler boomed.

"You might try to remember," Toby said, rising to indicate that the discussion was over, "that ours is a two-party system, though you might not always notice it. Anyway, why worry? I'm sure they won't come."

"There is that hope," Fansler said, brightening.

Janice Fansler, duly instructed by her husband, sent out the invitations, including one addressed to Mr. and Mrs. Reed Amhearst. She was perfectly aware that Kate had kept her own name, but she considered such attitudes trendy and foolish, and refused to notice them. Having sent the invitations and alerted the caterer who ran these functions for her, she put her mind to other things.

The invitation was addressed to Reed at the Columbia Law School, and he contemplated it with a certain wry amusement. He could hear Kate now, flatly refusing to attend. The question was, should he try to persuade her to accompany him?

Hours later, letting himself into the apartment, he decided to try. Kate, who was examining a telephone bill with the expression of bewilderment and horror characteristic of those engaged in such activities, offered him the fourteen pages of the document. "Has anyone considered carrier pigeons lately?" she asked.

"Your brother and sister-in-law, he of Darwin Darwin et cetera, have asked us to their annual party for the firm's associates. Might you consent to come, do you think?"

"You've been drinking," Kate said. "And before you even got home. A bad sign. Is the academic life more burdensome than the quiet, steady pace of things at the D.A.'s?"

"They've invited you as Mrs. Reed Amhearst. I thought maybe you could go as Kate Fansler, and observe how the other half lives. We can see the young, Fansler and other, which is always enlivening."

"I would have thought you met enough of the young at law school. Do bear in mind Jane Austen's descriptions of such parties: 'a mixture of those who had never met before and those who met too often.' Reed, I don't like to sound lawyerly myself, but didn't we agree, we might even call it a verbal contract, that we would not drag each other into our dreary social obligations? If you want to attend my brother's party, go, my child, and the Lord be with you, though in my view it marks the sad deterioration of a noble mind."

"One ought not, in middle age, to get into ruts, or to maintain, unexamined, the assumptions of one's youth. You have said it, and it's greatly to your credit."

"I didn't think you'd drag it up in connection with families. Because people are blood relations is no reason for intimacy — that was good enough for Margaret Mead, and it's good enough for me. Reed, is there some aspect to this I'm missing?"

"Connections between law professors and the big law firms are advantageous for all concerned when it comes to placing students and so forth."

"That I can see. Are these connections impossible to effect without a wife in hand?"

"My going alone would be a statement. Your coming along will be taken for granted. Besides, you always like seeing Leo and Leighton."

"Do they come to these legal dos? How the mighty are fallen. I know Leo's a lawyer, but don't tell me Leighton has gone that way too? Surely all my nieces and nephews are not going to be lawyers, just like my brothers."

"All the professional young attend this. If you'd ever behaved like a proper aunt, you'd know that."

"Reed, I don't mind telling you, I'm worried. You're going to be counsel for some big firm next, and giving parties yourself."

"I promise not. If this party is a nightmare, furthermore, I shall not try to persuade you again. So gamble one evening against a lifetime of discussion about one's duties to blood relations."

"You should go into the law," Kate said. "You have a flair for it."

Kate greeted her brother and sister-in-law in the acceptable manner by allowing them to place their cheek against hers. Her greeting to Leo and Leighton was warmer: a hug and smiles of pleasure.

"Find me a drink," Kate ordered, in her happiest autocratic manner, "a martini, of course, and sit down and tell me what you've been doing with yourselves."

"There aren't any martinis," Leighton said. "It's a Japanese feast, and you can have either Midori melon coolers or sake."

"To be followed," Leo said before she could ask, "by sushi, or California rolls, and I forget what else."

"My God," Kate said. "Well, see if you can find me some tomato juice. If one avoids mixed drinks of suspicious origin and soda pop, one can really find oneself sipping water at these affairs, and I haven't gone that far. Well, plain soda water, if all else fails, will do."

But Reed, who felt that, having dragged her here, he should see that she at least had a real drink, had found Scotch for her and himself. "What a relief," Kate said. "If one is going to give up drinking, one ought not to do it under this sort of pressure, don't you agree?" Reed smiled at her gratefully. At least Kate never sulked.

"What are you doing here, Leighton?" Kate asked. "Joined the yuppies when I wasn't looking?"

Leighton winced. "A yuppie is someone born after 1950 and before 1969 living in a city and earning over forty thousand dollars a year. I don't qualify on the last count. I earn three thousand dollars a year when I'm working, and came here because the family orders me to, Leo is here, and they even said you might come, not that I believed it."

"Still acting?" Kate asked.

"That's the hope. Meanwhile, like the others in my profession, I am either a waitress or a word processor. In my case it's word processing, for legal firms, at night. Very good pay, and leaves my days free."

"It's almost worth living on three thousand dollars a year if you ask me," Leo said. "I'm a yuppie by most common definitions, and I work all night and all day and all weekend. The only time you can be away from your desk without arousing the partners' suspicions is on Monday to Friday between nine and five. Then you might be somewhere on business or, in a pinch, at the dentist. But you damn well better be in your office in the evening and on weekends."

"Never mind all that," Leighton said, sitting down by her aunt. "Did you ever see a movie called *The Lady Vanishes?*" Kate nodded. "There's a wonderful piece of dialogue in it between the two cricket enthusiasts. One of them says to the other: 'She did, you know.' And the other says, 'Did what?' And the first says: 'Vanish.' That's what Leo and I want to talk to you about."

"I have a sense of dislocation, of being out of touch," Kate said.

"Leighton always starts in the middle of things," Leo said. "*In medias res.* It comes of having majored in Greek combined with excessive devotion to the plays of Ibsen. It's all quite simple and, in my opinion, uninteresting. Shall I tell it?" he asked Leighton. She nodded.

"But," she added, "I reserve the right to put in the dramatic details. Of which there are many." Kate listened to them with pleasure. She often pondered the ironic rewards of having had three impossible brothers — Larry, and the next two, who had produced, respectively, Leo and Leighton. Her tiresome older siblings had certainly paid off in the next generation.

"Toby," Leo continued, "got Leighton a job doing word processing, after she learned how."

"Not Uncle Larry?" Kate asked.

"Gimme a break," Leighton said.

"So," Leo said, "Leighton would arrive at six, and get her assignment from this woman who was in charge of the firm's word-processing room. One of those women without whom, not. You know. They're damn important, let me tell you, these word processors. The associate's future can depend on whether they do his or her work on time. Believe me, one keeps on the good side of the word processors, and the supervisor thereof. Partners never set foot in the Wang room, as we call it; they're always sending associates in there with work that's needed *immediately*. If an associate's not in good with the Wang room, forget it." Kate nodded her comprehension of all this.

"Well," Leo went on, "some months after Leighton started — she doesn't work steadily, you know, some weeks on, some weeks off, unlike us better-paid minions — she noticed this woman was gone. 'Sick,' Leighton was told. But the fact is, the woman never came back. And — "

"And," Leighton said. "That was the absolute last anybody anywhere heard of her. She was a damn nice woman."

"Everybody happy here?" Janice said, stopping off on her hostess rounds. "Can I get anybody anything?"

"Since you are so kind," Kate said, "might I have some Scotch ?"

Janice looked as though she were about to mention melon coolers, but apparently she changed her mind. It occurred to Kate, not without pleasure, that she was the only person in the room who had no reason to worry about offending Janice, or brother Larry if it came to that, with her demands. Janice nodded, and went off, apparently to summon a waiter. Kate waved Leighton on.

"I asked Toby," Leighton said, "and he said not to worry; people are always disappearing from law firms, particularly word processors and even supervisors. Not that the partners would notice unless a client disappeared. But this woman was particularly nice to me, you see, and I wondered."

Kate, accepting another Scotch from a waiter, smiled encouragingly at Leighton.

"And what, by the way, do you think her name is? Charlotte Lucas. Doesn't it sound made up?"

"Just because Jane Austen used it? Not necessarily," Kate said. "Made-up names sound made up because originally they were authentic. Take Merrill Ashley, the ballet dancer. Her name was Linda Merrill. Only another dancer named Linda Rosenthal took Linda Merrill as her name. So Merrill Ashley had to find the name Merrill Ashley. But 'Linda Merrill' is more like 'Charlotte Lucas,' don't you think? Improbable?"

Whether through the strange miracle of genes, or time spent in the company of this admired aunt, neither Leo nor Leighton responded to this analysis of nomenclature with the least bewilderment. "You're probably right," Leighton said. "As soon as something looks suspicious, everything looks suspicious; I've often noticed. Anyway, here's the odd thing. When I decided to talk to Toby, he completely changed the subject. Instead, do you know what he told me, in strictest confidence, of course?"

"Of course," Kate murmured.

"Well, I've only told Leo; and now you. Maybe it'll make sense to you. Years ago, Toby made a will for a woman writer. English and famous, is all Toby would say. She died, oh, ages ago, I don't know just when, and then another woman writer, also English and very scholarly, to whom the first woman had left everything, came to Toby and *she* made a will. Toby had been with another firm when he made the first will, and he brought the writer, the first one, with him when he came to Dar and Dar. Anyway, when the second one got in touch with him a short while ago, wanting to know if the will was all in order and would we be able to find the chief legatees, Toby couldn't find her — I mean one of the two legatees mentioned in the will. He could have found the woman's son, of course, but she knew where *he* was."

"Has this any connection with the disappearance of Charlotte Lucas?" Kate asked.

"Of course not," Leo said. "What possible connection could it have? Leighton is bored by word processing, for which who could blame her, and she's looking for excitement."

19

"Has Toby any interest in finding Charlotte Lucas?" Kate asked.

"I haven't talked to him about it again," Leighton said. "I've talked to you and Leo. But I do feel we should do something."

"Not, I trust," Kate said, "without consulting Toby."

"We thought," Leighton said, "you might consult him."

"Whyever?"

"Leo doesn't feel he should talk to Toby, being a young lawyer in another firm; he oughtn't to know about it. Etiquette, or whatever. And I don't think, as a mere word processor, I can push any more. I mean, it will really look as though I'm trying to make a scene. But you could just say to Toby, in a casual sort of way, that you heard about this and your detective instincts were aroused. Would you, Kate?"

"Probably not," Kate said. "But let me think about it. I'll let you know either way. I think I see our hostess headed this way to break up our little group. Very unpartyish, you know, having a confab."

"Leighton," Janice said. "Let me introduce you to one of the new associates in Larry's firm. From Harvard Law School. I told him you had gone to Radcliffe, and that you must have a lot in common."

Kate escaped before she heard Leighton's response to this. Leighton was very pretty indeed, but unfortunately, at least from the view of most Fanslers, bored to distraction by conventional young men. "I can always talk to Leo if I want the young lawyerly point of view," she had been known to say. Leo, in his turn, was now wafted off to be introduced elsewhere, and Kate wondered when dinner would be, and if, as Leo had threatened, it would be Japanese food, which was not one of her favorite ethnic repasts; Kate had never really come to terms with raw fish.

She spotted a comfortable sort of chair across the room, and headed for it. Leighton and Leo had made the early part of the evening agreeable; at dinner she would be placed somewhere by her sister-in-law, and would have to make conversation, or endure it, with some lawyer who, with any luck, would not know her connection to Reed and would say all sorts of delicious things she could treasure up for him. Meanwhile, she sought a solitary interlude. But scarcely had she achieved the chair when she was accosted by her brother. Having invited her, Larry felt, no doubt, the need to be minimally courteous, after his fashion.

"Well, Kate," he said, perching perilously on a nearby table. "How are things with you these days?" So, many years ago, Kate recalled, in that flash of memory so characteristic of middle age, he, home from Havard, had tried to question her, a schoolgirl. "Fine, Larry," she had said then, and said now.

"Glad you could come," he added, rising to his feet and patting her on the arm. "You seem to get on with the young better than I do," he added, making an insult of what might have been a compliment. "Well, at least the last presidential election showed they are coming to their senses. Not like that sixties generation. Quite a relief, isn't it?"

Kate nodded idiotically as he walked off. Somewhere, at some moment in their relationship, she had decided that Larry, that all her brothers, were not worth arguing with, a realization that filled her with sadness, and them, she did not doubt, with relief. To have realized the purposelessness of conversation was, for Kate, to have abandoned a relationship. Sometimes she wondered what, since she had no sisters, it might have been like to have a nice brother who offered her the kind of companionship she shared with Leo and Leighton. Count your blessings, she admonished herself. The young make better friends, and have the added advantage of surviving longer, so that we need not wait for their deaths to break our hearts. I knew I shouldn't have come, she told herself. Reed, it seemed, was making those connections so essential to the world of law in which he now moved. One had to know people; one had to appear one of them, even if one was not. Only then could one operate effectively.

But she had a pleasant surprise at dinner. She was seated next to Toby. "My manipulations, Kate," he said. "I hope you don't mind. I like to cheer Larry on through these capers of his for the benefit of the young, but when I heard you were coming I looked forward to tonight with more than my usual anticipation."

"It's good to see you," Kate said, "and I don't mind saying, a great relief. I thought I would have to talk to someone from bonds, on his way to being head of development for New London: uphill work all the way."

"You seem well informed on the doings of lawyers."

"My destiny, it appears. Brothers, husbands, now the next generation. I wonder when the eager young will go back to getting doctorates in the humanities. It's a different climate now, there's no question of that. But if I must talk to a lawyer, and that certainly seems inevitable tonight, I'm glad it's you."

Kate had met Toby when they were both youngish and still malleable, more malleable, it seemed to Kate, than the young were now. She mentioned this to Toby: "Or is that what everyone thinks as she grows old and disillusioned?"

"No," Toby said. "I think you're right. We knew the world we were living in wasn't much good, but that didn't stop us trying to change it. These young think that 'making it' is all there is. Perhaps because their doubts, if they had any, would be too profound to bear. I suspect that's it, don't you ?"

"Probably. But they will put up with my brother for what it gets them. You put up with him out of a combination of loyalty and charity; I do think there's a difference there. How, if it's not too madly tactless to ask, *do* you put up with him?"

But Toby was not to answer, not that evening. The woman on his other side demanded his attention, and Kate, as the result of some sort of signal inaudible to her, was simultaneously addressed by the man on her left. But before she and Toby parted at the end of dinner, they agreed to meet soon for lunch. Leighton's worries aside, Kate

24

thought it would be nice to talk to Toby again. She rather wondered what he had on his mind, besides the disappearance of Charlotte Lucas and some nameless English author.

Two

Early the next week Kate was surprised to discover Leighton waiting for her at the conclusion of her office hours. "Interesting bunch," Leighton said, as Kate let her into the office and shut the door. "I asked them what they thought of you, posing as another student. Opinions varied."

"Don't you think that was dishonest?"

"Probably. I am amoral and incurably curious. Haven't you noticed?"

"I've noticed that you're given to extravagant statements arising, I assume, from the dissatisfactions of your professional life."

"How do you know it's not the dissatisfactions of my personal life?"

"Elementary, my dear Watson. You are unlikely to consult me about your personal life: one's peers are the natural counselors for that,

26

not aunts. Secondly, I very much doubt you have problems with your personal life. You might have had, had you been young when I was. These days, I'd say you are one of those fortunate persons made for the time and place in which you live."

"Marvelous. I've always thought Holmes's deductions overrated, by the way. People who come to him always have scratched watches or ill health, or a habit of looking over their shoulders. He'd have made nothing of me. But I'm glad you mentioned Watson, because that's why I'm here."

"Leighton, what good news. They're doing a new play about Holmes, and have decided to make Watson a woman, casting you in the part. Or are you playing it in drag?"

"Kate, you are funny. It's not a play; I could have written a note about that. But I am about to play Watson, I hope. To your Holmes."

Kate stared at her niece. "My dear," she finally said when she had found her voice, "I know one's later twenties are a hard time of life. But many of the most accomplished people turn out, in their youths, to have had long periods of indecision. Have you read Erikson? Think of Luther, William James, Shaw, Yeats. There is no way you can cast me in the part of

Holmes. We have nothing in common except height and leanness. I haven't an aquiline nose, do not play the violin, have never tried cocaine or any other drug, drugs being the only part of modern life's revolution of which I heartily disapprove, am not English, and can't tell one cigarette ash from another, just for starters."

"You seem to know a lot about him."

"On the contrary, any Sherlockian would tell you I know nothing about him, except what I picked up as a child reading. Why in the world are we discussing Sherlock Holmes?"

"You're a woman; you're a detective, at least from time to time. You teach between cases — all Holmes did was play the violin and shoot up. It's not an important difference. What you lack, apart from fog, a wonderful landlady, and an ability at disguises, is Watson. Me. Now don't say something clever, just listen. You are at the beginning of a case; I can feel it. The disappearance of Charlotte Lucas. I shall chronicle it all. And, if my account catches on, as Watson's did, I'll write up your past cases. Have you ever noticed how many women came to see Holmes, and how good he was about getting them their rights?"

"Do you think Charlotte Lucas sleeps below a false vent, and is visited nightly by a dangerous snake who responds to whistles?"

"What a memory you have."

"Everyone remembers that. I suggest you attend a convention of Sherlockians, or Baker Street Irregulars, or whatever they call themselves, and really learn about memory and details. I was the merest idle peruser, and that eons ago. Leighton, hadn't we better talk about you?"

"What's to talk about? I appear in an occasional play, off-off-Broadway, sometimes just the work of apprentice playwrights. Have you ever wondered why the actors are always so much better than the plays? I do, all the time. As I already told you, to support myself I do word processing for legal firms. Tedium, and no fringe benefits, but the pay is good, and you can set your own schedule. I will say for the fancy law firms, they're always glad to have you. But working in the firm with Toby is preferable to working just anywhere. He's a nice man. I have the feeling he's in trouble; deep trouble."

"I have the feeling that you're writing a play, with Toby and me and you as the main characters. Why not run off and do it?"

"What about Charlotte Lucas and the English author? Kate, promise to have lunch with Toby, and get him to confide in you. Then you can tell me all about it."

"That is a thoroughly immoral suggestion."

"Nonsense. He's not going to tell you he's murdered anyone. I only mean, let me in on the beginning of the case."

"Leighton, I'm tired and I'm going home. There is no case, and if there were, the last thing I need is a Watson."

"Everyone needs a Watson. If we each had a Watson, none of us would need a therapist, psychiatrist, or confessor. Had you thought of that?"

"That's probably a profound observation. As it happens, however, I need none of the above."

"Exactly why I chose you. Kate, do please cooperate. Let's just start with Toby. If after you see him, you want to tell me to go away and play, I'll go. But let's wait till then. Okay?"

And Kate, torn between bewilderment, annoyance, and amusement, agreed. After all, what could Toby possibly tell her?

Toby, offering her lunch at the Harvard Club, made Kate wonder, before they were well past their appetizer, whether Leighton ought not to be Holmes. For Toby was very troubled indeed. Kate, searching for a light note of diversion, asked why the Harvard Club had the head of a dead elephant nailed to the wall of the lounge. "Not enough leather on the chairs?" she asked.

"You haven't seen the portraits: presidents of the United States who went to Harvard, presidents of Harvard, presidents of the Harvard Club. Is there anyone else in the world? If that had been the last head of the last elephant in the world, what better destiny than to adorn the high walls of the Harvard Club ?"

"I don't know what to say, Toby; you're stealing my lines."

"How is Reed liking his new job?"

"Very much, I think. He says the academic life, in its higher reaches, is the most relaxed and satisfying he knows, and he was right to want to taste it before the old order changeth."

"The old order has changed in law firms. Even in litigation, they work for big companies warding off suits by individuals they've injured; not that the big corporations are wrong to defend themselves, but some of the suits like DES or asbestos are so repugnant not even the most ambitious associates want to work on them. Or the law firms are involved in one company's taking over another

31

company to no one else's particular benefit, perhaps with greenmail, golden parachutes, who knows what. It just doesn't seem worth the sixteen-hour days of marvelously intelligent men and women."

"My dear, you sound like Leo."

"Of course I do; Leo is right."

"Why don't the big companies just settle the suits?"

"Because it might encourage millions of others to make small suits of the same kind. That can run into money."

"Surely, Toby, this isn't getting you down after all these years." Kate, looking at him, was worried. Toby was one of those people who had always been around. He had been to Harvard with one of her brothers, not Larry, and somehow had stayed part of the family, rather, she thought, like that chap in *Brideshead Revisited* who was always present when anything happened. Kate had loved the beginning of that BBC series, and hated the end, as she had hated the end of the book. But Toby, unlike his *Brideshead* counterpart, had stayed attractive to the end. Perhaps, Kate thought, watching the waiter change plates, and taking one of the popovers, which were, Toby had told her, very good, he had never got over his wife's death. She had been killed on New Year's Eve returning from a party Toby had cut because he had the flu. She was hit by a drunken driver going eighty in the wrong lane. Kate had not known much about his marriage, had never particularly warmed to his wife; it occurred to her now that she had seen remarkably little of him in the past few years.

"I've grown in the habit of talking about things that don't matter, even with great animation," he said. "Because it seems too long since I've talked to anyone about anything that mattered. I don't mean the law, of course. And, egoist that I am, I don't mean other people's problems. Since the younger partners and the associates can hardly talk to Larry about anything, they tend to talk to me — I come next on the letterhead."

"And you're damn good at being talked to. I know the syndrome," Kate said. "It all comes in, and nothing goes out. And if I hadn't Reed to talk to. . . . You never thought of marrying again?"

"Kate, that's what I want to talk to you about. And don't ask, 'Why me?' When Larry spoke to me about inviting you to his blasted party, I suddenly realized: Of course, I shall talk to Kate. Why didn't I think of it? I used to chat with Leighton, and thought of you often, but it took Larry's bumbling remarks to make me realize you were just what I needed. Of course I thought of marrying again. But at the moment, I'm living with Charlotte Lucas."

"The one who's disappeared?"

"The same. Except she hasn't disappeared. That was a little plan that went awry." Toby moved the food on his plate, and then put his fork down. "You can't imagine what it was like after Patricia was killed. I mean, she was gone. I won't say we had one of the great marriages in the world, if there are any great marriages, but it worked, as they say, and we jogged along. I labored long hours; she played the cello and studied languages after the children were grown. You know the sort of thing, though how you escaped it was always one of the wonders to me. Suddenly, she was gone. There was no one there when I came home. There was no one who knew who Larry was, who could make a fuss about going to a party for the associates. My God, Kate, you must know what I mean. My sons, and especially their wives, were nice enough, and kept inviting me over on Sundays, but it was perfectly clear I would have to get married again. I know it's supposed to be very easy for men. And perhaps it is, if you're the least bit of a swinger. I'm not. It isn't as though, at fifty-five, I was out on the prowl for someone to go to bed with. It would have been nice to have someone in my bed on a regular basis, but what I needed was a leisurely, established relationship. I've found in the last year that everything takes more time, including sex, which isn't bad. I wonder sometimes why I was always rushing, always impatient. I like to get there now, but if I get there a half-hour later, fine."

"You didn't feel like playing the dating, mating game?"

"I didn't. And I was lonely as hell. There used to be times when Patricia was away, and I rather enjoyed them, to tell you the truth. But how long were they? A couple of weeks, at most. I hadn't thought, of course, how much I just wanted someone being part of the place where I lived. It wasn't, as people used to suggest, the laundry, or the dishes, or arranging things with the cleaning woman. It was calling out to say something when there was no one there to hear it." Kate nodded.

"Then Charlie came into the office. Charlotte Lucas, to you. She came in originally to inquire about an author whose will I made up years ago, not the one whose will I still have, though they are connected: they were friends

— not the wills, the authors." Toby smiled. "The wills were too, I guess."

"Toby, you're becoming more elliptical with the years. I didn't pause over those golden parachutes, but you'd better run the bit about how Charlotte Lucas came to the office past me once more, slowly."

"All Charlie's life she has wanted to write a biography of Charlotte Stanton — the writer, you know — and the first woman whose will I drew up, years ago. Good biographers are good detectives, as Charlie says, and when she found out about that will, she came to the office to see me. She's still working on the biography, by the way, and she's still seeing me."

"Why did an English author make a will in America?"

"Ah, now you're the detective at work. Not worrying about my sad love life; on to a clue."

"It is a rather obvious question," Kate said.

"With a rather obvious answer: she was in America, lecturing, and learned she was ill. She didn't want to chance dying here, leaving only the will she had made a long time ago. May I go on with the story of my love life?"

Kate smiled. "I can see," Toby said, "you're still pondering the will, but I'll come back to it, I promise. It's part of why I wanted to see you, in fact, but only part. And as far as

I'm concerned, we're talking about me, or I am, and that hasn't happened for a very long time. I was thinking of hiring someone to listen as I told my story. Not a psychiatrist or anything, just another human being. But one who might understand. That's when I thought of you. Look duly flattered. Anyway, Charlie and I went out to dinner to continue talking about her author, and it was the first time I'd been relaxed with a woman who really seemed to want to talk about a subject, and not take part in a mating dance whose steps I had forgotten. Oh, there are very attractive women lawyers at Dar and Dar. But they're part of the firm, and I felt too senior for that. I did think of cultivating some woman lawyer in another firm, but I hadn't got round to it. Charlie came along. Are you in a hurry? We could have some coffee in the lounge, under the elephant's head."

Once in the lounge, Kate sank into a deep leather chair; had she been an inch shorter, she thought, her legs would not have reached the ground unless she sat forward. She pictured generations of women guests, on the rare occasions when they were welcomed in the old days, perched on the edge of huge chairs, regarding a stuffed elephant head. "Go on," she said.

"I'll skip the author part, for the moment. We'd taken to going out and talking, about authors and other things, and then Charlie said she needed a job to make money. I was gallant enough to suggest living on me; I made enough money for two. But being independent was very important to her. As it happened, the woman who had been supervising our Wang room left, and Charlie told me she'd supported herself by office work for years, and would I mind if she interviewed for the job. To be frank, I didn't think for a moment the partners would hire Charlie, simply because she was a writer in my eyes, and because she seemed so young to me; she's in her thirties. But she had a good track record and makes a very good impression, and she got the job. Why didn't we tell people at the firm we were, as they used to say, going together? God knows. The remnants of gentlemanly discretion? A natural bent for secrecy on both our parts? When we decided to live together, we didn't tell anyone either, not even my sons. They're of the generation that thinks it perfectly natural we were living together, but my being, as you will have understood with your great detective instincts, a basically old-fashioned guy, I didn't want to have our relationship bruited about the office, especially since

Charlie was planning to leave before too long to work on her biography. She was saving up to support her research, as she put it."

"Toby. Are you happy with her? Was deciding to live with her secretly a good idea? You don't look happy, and I want you to be happy. If you're miserable, say so please."

"Charlie has made me very happy. Odd, isn't it, that I didn't make that clear. I'm already taking her . . . it . . . our relationship, for granted, which is the best of all. Like health, you want it so you don't have to think about it. I rather wish your niece hadn't started all this business about Charlie's disappearing. I used, when young, to have a great-aunt who called all children she liked "bright-eyed and bushy-tailed," and I remember thinking if she said that I again, I would go out and find a bushy tail and swat her with it, but that's how Leighton was: bright-eyed and bushy-tailed. The only comfort is, so far no one knows but you, and Leighton, and Leo."

"True enough; but we may have to let Leighton play Watson to keep her from making more trouble. Leighton is responsible, when trusted: I do feel confident of that. But if I say, 'I can't tell you anything,' in pompous tones, she will probably go on investigating, and who is to blame her? On the other hand, we can hardly tell her what we're investigating when we don't know what it is. Or do we?"

"Do I sense a bargain? If I let Leighton play Watson, you'll at least listen to me? But do use discretion with Leighton. She must either do her word processing in another office or pretend she doesn't know me. I can't live much longer with these deep looks from underneath her long lashes."

"You seem better already, Toby. It must be the vibes from the elephant's head. Why do I assume that he was a male elephant?"

"Because they didn't let women into the Harvard Club except under the most stringent rules. They certainly didn't pin them to the walls. Kate, will you come and talk to Charlie and me together? We wish to hire you as a private detective in a case on which we are engaged. And I can't say anything more; one is forbidden to do business at the Harvard Club. As everyone knows, these clubs are purely for social purposes."

"I'd love to meet Charlie," Kate said. "May I tell Reed you're living together?"

"I seem to be relying rather heavily on all your relatives," Toby said. "All right. But for God's sake don't tell Larry."

"I haven't told Larry anything since I was

five years old," Kate said. "Why would I?"

Kate did not hear from Toby about a meeting with him and Charlie. Just as she was beginning to decide that Toby had regretted his confidences — in her experience, a not uncommon result of uncharacteristic intimacy — she found Charlie waiting for her, as Leighton had done, at the end of her office hours.

Charlie introduced herself. "Toby and I thought it would be better if we started by letting you see the documents," she said, after she had seated herself, and the proper amenities had been observed. "I decided, in order not to take any more advantage of you than absolutely necessary, to come during your office hour and wait at the end of the line."

"Did you ask the students what they thought of me?"

"God, no," Charlie said. "Should I have?"

"Hardly. I just wanted to reassure myself that there are certain impulses one outgrows. You've met my niece, Leighton, of course. She too waited one day outside my office door. Has Toby grown shy again?"

"Not really," Charlie said. "Well, maybe, a bit. But the truth is, when he and I started going over this whole thing, we realized that the documents were all here. Enough of them, that is, to get you started on the problem, at least, to enable you to understand what the problem is. We did hire a private detective, by the way, a man who's given up on the job. But he's a nice man, and he said he'd be glad to tell you what he found: mostly negatives, I think, but that's worth something."

"If he failed, why on earth should I succeed? I have less time, less experience, and probably fewer contacts in the world of investigations."

"True. Toby and I discussed all that thoroughly. He even went to England, this chap, and can tell you all about his investigations there. We'll have to pay him his hourly rate to talk to you, but it will be worth it. We think that someone who understands the sort of woman Winifred was, and someone who is herself a woman, might do better. You do seem to have a sort of flair for this sort of thing."

"Who is Winifred?"

"Winifred Ashby is the honorary niece of Charlotte Stanton, who was a famous author and principal of an Oxford college."

"Of course," Kate said. "She wrote all those immensely popular novels about ancient Greece, Ariadne and Hippolyta."

"The very same. No, I shan't say any more. I'll simply leave all these things, if you feel up to it. I just happened to bring them with me."

Kate smiled. Charlie was a woman who might, by now, be nearing forty, pleasant-looking, immediately likable. She had short, wavy red hair, and was plump with a "this is how I am, and aren't I pleasant to be with" air. It was not hard, Kate thought, to sense her attractions for Toby. His wife had been meticulously turned out always, with a certain rigidity of manner and an edge to her voice that was no easier to listen to because it was probably unconscious. She and Toby had worked out, as do most couples, a *modus vivendi:* they got along, they got by. But with Charlie, Kate guessed, things were easier, more unexpected, more fun, but also more dangerous.

"I thought we'd just leave you these. Then, when you've read them, we can have a long consultation, you and me and Toby." She placed on the desk before Kate one of those heavy paper folders, full. "What you have here is Winifred's journal, or at least the piece of it that was later found on the farm. In addition to Winifred's journal, there are all the letters I wrote to Toby from Massachusetts and while I was in England with Winifred. They're only slightly edited to delete matters having nothing to do with the case. I think they give you a pretty good idea of what was going on. Later, I can fill in any mysterious gaps; I don't think there are many."

Charlie rose. "These are copies, by the way. We've kept all the originals, so you needn't worry about these — except, of course, that they're frightfully confidential. So you won't mention any of this to Leighton, will you? At least, not yet. Toby told me about that problem, and I do understand; I like Leighton. But just for now, in case you want to say 'Forget it,' or 'I think this is a case for the police,' or something, I'd rather you didn't discuss it all with anyone."

Kate sat for a while after Charlie had left. She could, by now, recognize the last moment when she might, with decency, turn back, not go forward. Well, she thought, I'll read the stuff. Then, gathering up her new folder, her old briefcase, her purse, and her general sense of end-of-day confusion, she headed for home.

Three

WINIFRED'S JOURNAL

I had always known that one day I would be found out, yet when the visitors turned up I was unsuspecting and unprepared. Like anyone with a secret, I had allowed even a short passage of time to assuage my fear of discovery.

Ted told me about them at the time, and I can now reconstruct the scene with the knowledge of hindsight as though I had been there. They would have followed directions from the town, counting the houses and noticing the mailboxes, but they had been told it was the first farm they would come to, so that part was not too difficult. They must, indeed, have wondered where to look, in the barn, or the house, or the fields — they entered the barn, Ted said, as though they had wandered onto a movie set. Or perhaps their idea of farmers was left over from an earlier time. Ted was mixing up powdered milk for the calves, and preparing to feed the pigs he is raising this year, and the pigs were squealing. The cows had not too long since been milked, and I render up for myself the smell that must have greeted the visitors: warm milk, poured out for the cats; urine; manure; pig — though clean pigs smell a lot less than everyone supposes. Ted said the visitors stepped into some manure the spreader had not yet got to; I'm glad of that, anyway.

"We're looking for Winifred Ashby," they said.

"Not here," Ted said laconically. He tries to act like a rube if city types give him the chance. Ted's grandfather used to own this farm, and he grew up on it, but he's no rube, and his wife is no rube either. But as summer people have bought up the farms hereabouts, Ted and Jean amuse themselves with playing the fool. It does no one any harm, I suppose, and in this case, I'm glad he did.

"Is your name Ted Wilkowski?" they asked.

"Always has been," Ted said. He finished mixing the milk for the vealers, and started carrying it out to them in the boxes they occupy by the side of the barn. The male calves are raised for veal, and they're kept pretty confined in their boxes until they're sold. But the boxes are big enough for them to stand up, or lie down out of the sun, and they have some wire-enclosed space outside the boxes, so it's not as cruel as it might be. I don't like it, but a farm is no place for sentimentalists about animals. The visitors were forced to follow Ted outside, into a good deal of mud, if they wished to continue talking to him, and, after exchanging a meaningful glance, they did so. Ted knew I didn't welcome people, and he wasn't going to offer undue encouragement. "The woman we're looking for," they said, "she's not a very young woman. We were told she lived here with you, on this farm, and worked here."

"Now, who might've told you that?" Ted asked.

The visitors realized by now that they were getting nowhere. "Is there a woman who lives and works here?" they asked.

"Several," Ted said. "There's my wife, but she's not here. There's my hired man, but she's not here. There's my wife's mother, but she's not here either. My mother lives down the road a piece; she helps out from time to time."

Ted swears he said "down the road a piece," having got carried away with his role, but

I rather doubt that.

"Did you say your hired man's a woman?" they asked.

"I didn't exactly say, but she is."

"What is her name?" they asked.

"Well now," Ted said, "I reckon I'm not going to tell you that. You just wait till you find her, and you ask her yourselves any questions you got. But I'd be careful if I was you; she's got a pretty fierce temper."

Then they got in their car and drove away, turning around in the barnyard. Just before they reached the car, one of Ted's geese waddled up; the woman held out her hand to it, and it bit her, I'm glad to say, though not badly. Of course, that wouldn't scare them away for long. But I was glad to know I had a substitute on the premises, acting as I would have liked to, had I been there.

"Whatever it is you've done," Ted said to me that evening, "I'm afraid they've tumbled to it. I acted as much like an escaped lunatic, rural variety, as I dared, but I think they've only gone as far as their motel, to regroup. Do you owe them money?"

"I don't owe them anything," I said. "Or anyone else either. When I told you I had committed no crime, injured no one, that was the simple truth. All they want is to ask me questions. Maybe to do with a writer who's still famous these days, someone I used to know." (Did I believe that then?) "And I don't want to talk about her; that's all there is to it."

"Somehow it reminded me of the FBI coming after a longsought criminal, in old movies."

I laughed, knowing what he meant. Most people like to fit things into stories they already know; it makes them feel a bigger part of life than they are. Writers do this more than most people. Why do I say that? Because I understand, being a sort of writer myself. What marks a writer is this: until she — or he, of course — writes down whatever happened, turns it into a story, it hasn't really happened, it hasn't shape, form, reality. I think so many women keep diaries and journals in the hope of giving some shape to their inchoate lives.

"Well," Ted said, "I don't want any trouble. You know that."

"Have I given you any?"

"Not yet. But there isn't a hired man I've ever had who didn't give me trouble in the end."

I knew that was true. It was why Ted kept on with our arrangement. Being a hired hand is about the hardest work there is, the loneliest, and the worst paid. But that is partly because most hired hands can't work out their own deals, not knowing what they want. I had known.

I had searched out Ted's farm and its routine and conditions with great care, having made up my mind that work on a farm was what I wanted: hard work, but not all day, even if every day. That's the thing about cows. When I first rented a small house here, I didn't know much about cows, though I had romantic ideas about farming. Romantic, in my lexicon, means unreal, glossed over with a false attractiveness to entrap those who will not see through the gloss to the truth beneath. Advertising is wholly dependent on romance; so is the position of women in our society, or (to take an example of male romance in the United States) the life of cowboys. You take the worst feature of the life — subservience for the wife, isolation for the cowboy — and you glamorize it, you give the wives or cowboys the language in which to describe to themselves the romance of their situation.

I used to be romantic about loneliness, about living alone and having nothing to do but write and read, no demands to meet, no superficial society, no chitchat, no tiresome job. Perhaps those utterly in the throes of their art find such solitude productive. I read once of a philosopher, Suzanne Langer, who went away to an isolated cabin in the woods to finish a book. I can understand that, the surge of energy required to get onto paper the ideas slowly formed, slowly learned. But solitude works, I suspect, only in special cases. Simenon, for example, used to shut himself up for the ten days it took him to write a Maigret novel. Of course, his loving wife, his well-trained household, left his food at his door and cleaned his bathroom. I understand now there are colonies — MacDowell, Yaddo — that provide such service and solitude for those large with book or concerto. But for all these, the point was they were famous: demands were made upon them. Solitude meant escape from the importuning of strangers. I was, at the time I first settled down alone, as unimportuned as a human being can well be.

When I first came here to Massachusetts I began to notice cows. They lined up each day at about four or earlier — they lined up also in the morning; no, not lined up, crowded round, though they knew their order, they knew their time to be serviced, but it was to be a while before their morning actions involved me — and milk was extracted from, unlikely as it seemed, a hundred cows, more or less. I walked to farms, I spied on them. There was one farmer on the road I knew I would never work for. He had no real use for animals; he treated them with just that added degree of indifference for living things that is a fine line, but unmistakable. But he liked to talk, and I found, as he harrowed, or sprayed, or planted the fields near me, that if I came out with iced coffee, he would stop to drink it and hold forth. Everyone likes to talk shop, which is the most interesting talk in the world, in the beginning.

Two compelling facts about dairy farming declared themselves: the cows had to be milked morning and night, every day, no exceptions, ever. And you had to know how to work and fix machinery. If every time a tractor, hay elevator, milker, cooler broke down you had to wait for a repairman, you would be out of business in a week. Some machinery, collapsed, required professional attention, but on a day-to-day basis one had to understand the internal combustion engine, simple mechanics, and electricity, if one was to be any use on a dairy farm. With the joy of a new commitment and a schedule, I set out to learn the mechanics. My small income went to taking courses in mechanics; I was smart, concentrated, and I read. The other students were young, their attention still diffuse. Thus, if I stayed late to tinker, even to ask questions, I was not disdained. Machines are often endowed by their owners with personality, but in fact, they have none: only inherent defects or strengths that are unchanging. I liked machines, partly for this, and partly because caring for them was not "woman's work." If men's superior strength had ever been a factor, it was no longer. The machines had the muscles, strength beyond that possessed even by the strongest man; one provided patience and mechanical skill. In exchange one found a firm schedule, and a lonely life, rural, camouflaged.

The beauty of the world around me mattered most of all, but do not look for an account of that here. I was amused to read once, in an interview with Joseph Campbell, who had written on myths and archetypal stories, that he knew himself not to be a novelist. "You know," he told an interviewer, "a novelist has to be interested in the way things look, the way the light falls on your sleeves and that kind of thing. That's not my talent and I found that everything I did was stiff and I quit." I am amused and envious of those who go to live alone, and write of how a cardinal feeds its mate, or of how a raccoon comes to the door, or of the mixed pathos and joy of trees against the sky just before the light fails. But I, committed to solitude and a rural life, write only of civilization, which I, with fascination, hate. My love for nature is full of pain and fear for its demise.

I approached Ted, and Ted's wife, with care. My greatest hurdle, I knew, was that they would think me mad, not worth chancing, probably devoted to secret vices. My strength was that I provided the kind of help almost wholly unavailable to farmers. I had to make the hope outweigh the fear. And I had to be certain to make my own claims clear from the beginning. I worked it all out as though I were infiltrating their lives, as the FBI does. I was canny and patient.

Ted had put up for rent a house on his land. It was too close to the farm, and too lacking in amenities, to be rented for long, but hunters took it in November to slaughter deer, and skiers took it sometimes when they could get nothing better. It was an A-frame, built for some family reason, when Ted's grandfather still ran the farm. A-frames were a big thing in the late '60's. They were easily put up, had high "cathedral" ceilings, a bath and kitchen. The sleeping area was a loft built over the back half of the main room, and this detracted from the appeal of the place for all but the young and active. One had to climb a rather tall ladder to go to bed, or else sleep in the living/dining area. I like heights and space; I liked the pointed ceiling, though because of it, the house cost more to heat than anyone could have foreseen when it was designed. Big trees stood near it, shading it: I liked the fact that Ted's grandfather had preserved them, not just bulldozed the site, as most did. The cabin I had been occupying was cramped, and cheap, and its paint was peeling. I had begun to dream of Ted's A-frame house, and to plan my life in it. I visited Ted and his wife (which is how I thought of her then, an appendage to him but one with power, one to be assuaged and reassured) one evening after their dinner. I had telephoned first. Evening is the only time you can have a conversation with a farmer, unless you follow him, or her, into the barn or onto a field. They are tired; they won't stay up late with you, but their attention is available. I had said on the telephone only that I wanted to talk to them about something; I intended, I succeeded, in taking them wholly by surprise.

Ted's wife was named Jean; I had seen her once or twice in the supermarket, moving with ease, rangy, comfortable in her farm clothes, not done up. I liked that. She and I understood each other in an instinctive way from the first. I've tried to describe this to myself, but like most intuitive perceptions, it evades description. I shall get it down one day. We did not fear one another, we did not need to protect our masks from one another: that's as close as I can come. I think it turned the balance in favor of my proposition; anyway, it helped.

I had worked my plan out carefully, on paper, which impressed them, and frightened them a little, as I meant it to. I wanted them to be, and to remain, a bit in awe of me.

"It's not a legal contract," I said. "I just wanted to list my demands, and offerings, and let you respond with yours. There will have to be a trial period. I may tell you I am strong and efficient and reliable, but you'll have to find that out for yourselves. What I will offer to do is this: I'll take total charge of the milking every morning. I'll do the afternoon milking also, or, if you prefer, I'll do whatever has to be done in the fields during the time I would be milking. I can run machinery: I can harrow, plant, spray, cut corn, cut grass for daily feedings. That's all I shall work: three hours in the morning, three hours in the late afternoon. I don't want to be asked to take on any extra work. If you want to go away for a day, a week, and leave me with both milkings, you'll have to find someone else to do the rest of the work. I want that to be clear. I shall work only the time both milkings take.

"In exchange, I want to live in your A-frame; it shall be my home, I shall care for it, and you will not enter it when I am there. In addition, you'll pay me fifty dollars a week." I had thought this amount out with great care. It would, together with my small income, keep me. I hoped it would leave me below the income-tax line. I wanted to keep what I got, and to count on it. Those were my terms, neither more nor less on either side.

"I don't expect you to decide now," I told them. "Perhaps we should say, if you agree to try, that either of us can end it on a week's notice anytime in the first three months. I may be awkward at the milking at first, but I shall improve fast. It gives you a certain freedom you wouldn't otherwise have. It gives me hard work each day, a good place to live, and time between the work for writing, which is what I do." I didn't want them to wonder about me too much.

I finished the coffee they had offered me and left. I walked home down the road, hoping, even expecting that the bargain would go through. I had presented them with a very great temptation, and I thought I had picked the right farmer. He was not uneducated, which meant he was not irrationally suspicious. The idea of a woman no longer young taking on hard, physical work was certainly unusual, but his wife would counter any fear of that. She, as I had guessed and was to learn for certain, detested "woman's work." When the children were young she would hire someone, if need be, to leave them with, and herself drive the tractor. Now the children were often with her in the summers as she worked in the fields, a boy and girl the same size, close in age. They, too, had been part of my reckoning. I do not like children, but allowed to retain my dignity, I can deal with them on equal terms. The night had been dark as I left their bright parlor, but soon my eyes grew attuned to the gentler night light; there was a moon, in the cool March evening. I was joyful with one of those surges of happiness that mark the beginning of an enterprise, when we believe we have got our life into some kind of order, and have the guts to see it through, even the hard times.

I moved into the A-frame a week later.

I had not, of course, really been inside of it

before, only peeked through the windows when I knew the farm was deserted. The Labradors they kept as pets and watchdogs barked furiously at me, but I had walked by so often, and showed so little fear of them, that in time they accepted me as having a right to be around the place. Inside, the A-frame looked even better: its walls were stained wood; no peeling paint. I liked the darkness; there was sun enough outside. Someone had added a porch I did not like to the front, but I learned to pile wood there; also, it was a place to leave my muddy farm boots, so even that worked out. The bathroom, Ted told me with pride, had ceramic tile. He had had to dig a well for the A-frame, having hoped that the spring would be sufficient, but in dry summers, the water ran out. The well diggers had gone down three hundred feet before they found water, and then only on the second time, a dowser having been called in. It amused me that they trusted dowsers too little to use them the first time, but they always called them in when the first time failed, and then the diggers found water. I was amused, but I agreed: one does not call on magic too soon, or carelessly, nor on hidden powers.

"Perhaps I better milk with you the first two times," Ted said, challenging me.

I did not take up the challenge, being too old to play the fool. "I would be grateful," I said. "I have studied the milking-parlor process" — I saw him smile at the verb — "and I know I can do it in time. The weight of the machines is not the problem. But if you can help me get into the routine, I shall be better at it sooner."

Ted shrugged. I'm sure he figured this wouldn't work out, but he had little to lose (no one was then renting the A-frame) and though I was a long shot, if I did work out. . . . We began the day after I moved in.

It didn't take us long to see that we had, they on their part and I on mine, found a human wonder; our culture can speak of it only in terms of heterosexual love, romance, marriage, but friendship too has its miracles, and the companionship of work perhaps more. I freed them from that essential bit of a hard life perhaps too demanding, allowing them a life with just enough maneuver room to allow them to dream. I was thorough in my work and, after a short enough time, efficient. They left me alone. They never tried to enter my home, or to look at it when I was not there. I know that, because I had rigged up devices to tell. They won my trust slowly, more slowly than I won theirs. When the visitors came, Ted was as much on my side as a schoolboy in an English story. We were buddies, we were allied against the others. I had found a friend.

Four

WINIFRED'S JOURNAL

The first time I found a friend I was eight years old, and in England on what was to be an annual visit. I was sent to Oxford to stay with an aunt — I understood from the beginning that the title was honorific — for all of my American school vacation. Why this began when I was eight, and not before, I was not told. My aunt was a tutor at an Oxford college for women; the English long vacation does not coincide with the American one, which was based, originally, on agricultural needs that freed American students in time for work on the farm. So that when I arrived at Oxford, the Trinity term was still under way. I had been delivered there by a kindly gentleman who had kept an eye on me on the ship, and completed the kindness (for which I now realize he was paid, but his kindness was no less for that) by accompanying me first to London and then moving me and my several bags from Waterloo to Paddington and onto the Oxford train; when we arrived, finally, at the Oxford station, he delivered me, by bus, to a house on the Woodstock Road.

My aunt was not at home, but the owner of the house, from whom my aunt rented a self-contained apartment, expected me. It was with her and her husband and son I was actually to stay. She greeted me with a casual understanding of a child's need to be attended to with care and yet offhandedly. (I realize now that it is the manner I assume with Ted and Jean's children, with what success I do not know: different times, different children, different place. I have often heard it said that the one mistake parents never make with their own children is the mistake their parents made with them. Perhaps those of us who are childless treat children in the light of gifts of love we received when young.) She told me about herself, and her husband — a don at Oxford, and rarely home — and her son, a boy my age. He was a day boy at the Dragon School, a preparatory school in Oxford, and as I ate my bread and jam, perched on a stool, he came in. Were I given to the language, the one most ready to our use, of romantic love, I would say I fell in love with him at that first moment. But this would not be true. Often we women (and the opposite, for all I know, may be true of men) think we have fallen in love with men when we have only fallen in love with the experience of being male in our world. I am certain that a large part of Rochester's attraction for Jane was the experience he had had of the world, sexual and other. What he had to offer her was an account of that experience. Which was what Cyril offered me.

I remember best of all how he was dressed, and the longing born in me at that moment for clothes like that. Many years later I read of a famous woman writer who had had, through the loss of a trunk, to wear her brother's clothes, and that the freedom of that time lived with her always. It was not just the freedom of the clothes, but their style: they combined, to my envious eye, comfort and evidence of community. He wore short gray flannel trousers, with knee socks, a shirt and tie, and a jacket with his school's emblem on the pocket. I took this in all at once, as one is said to do in the lyrics of popular songs of the twenties and thirties: "I took one look at you," and so on. It seemed to me in an instant that to be a boy like that, in such a school in

England, was to be the most fortunate creature on earth.

I have since pondered the lot of the upper classes, and the ghost of ancient customs that still remained for certain privileged boys after World War II. I am, I daresay, as widely read as most on the Orwell generation and those that followed. I understand the outrageous privilege, the unquestioned right — the arrogance, if you will — of such boys, following their inevitable path from preparatory school to public school to University, living a life on ancient turf, to the sound of cricket balls smacked in long summer afternoons, and bells, and the rooks circling around the spires. This was my romance, formed, no doubt, from readings about Edwardian England and the golden summer afternoons; it was all embodied for me in a single moment by the entrance of Cyril that day in June.

What his loneliness was that made him willing to be my friend I never asked, even of myself, not then. Had I been a boy, I would have been a threat; as a girl, I was none. Even if, as it turned out, I did most things better than he, even boyish, athletic, daring things, his being a boy made him naturally superior; he could allow me that satisfaction. And since I was there only for the summer — we did not, that first time, know that it would be every summer, but even when we did, summers are not years — I did not challenge his place in the family, with his parents, even with my "aunt." She, for example, though she had been taught Latin as a child, accepted his drilling in that honored language, and simply scoffed at my ignorance of such things. Like so many women I was to meet in future years, she did not expect for other females the privileges she had earned as an exception to women's inadequate destiny. But I determined at that moment that she could expect them of me. Cyril was willing enough to "teach" me — which is to say he lent me his Latin book and himself read the *Boys' Own* paper. (Once back in the States, I did, in fact, find a Latin teacher, and pursued my studies as far as Virgil, whom I can still read; more, I can recite — at least the passage where the Trojans leave the horse. My anger at Dido is such that I have never been able to memorize that passage, and even my aunt, flippantly assigning other women to the domestic sphere she despised, thought Dido a fool, I suppose because Dido's job was to rule a kingdom.) I did not yet know how many heroines there were, from Maggie Tulliver to Ursula Brangwen, who would think that a knowledge of the

66

classics would bring them into the mysterious male realm of power; if one learns the priestly language, may one not have access to the priestly mysteries?

Latin, however, mattered less than clothes. Even today, old as I am, if challenged to name the perfect moment of my life, the clearest in its passionate intensity, I would name the moment when Cyril let me wear his school clothes — the long leave had begun — and go about with him all day dressed as a boy, taken everywhere for a boy. (Cyril's hair was, in the English fashion, as long as mine.) His pockets were deep, and held more than I had thought of carrying. To plunge my hands into them was ecstasy. I could move in any way I wanted; sit with my legs apart. We went, I remember, to Blenheim, taking the bus — it was a favorite journey of ours — and scooted in and out of the buildings and gardens. I have never known such pure happiness.

He did not let me wear his clothes again; indeed, had his mother found out, eventually his father, there would have been the devil to pay for both of us. And I had had to promise to serve him as his vassal all summer in payment of his great daring. But perhaps because I had worn the clothes that day — passed, one might say, as a boy — he allowed me to join with his group of friends when, upon occasions that were rare enough, they played some game over the summer. I pleaded with my aunt to buy me a boy's outfit to wear; she could not fail to see that my clothes were unsuitable to my life. We went, I remember, to an outfitters, and I got an English girl's school uniform: like Cyril's, except for the skirt and hat. It was far better than nothing; I should never have found the courage to ask in the store for the trousers I wanted, even short trousers like Cyril's, even if I had not known such a request would have profoundly shocked my aunt. (There is a portrait of her in the College where she was Principal, wearing her academic gown and a tie. But the tie is knotted just above her breasts, as though in acknowledged compromise, just below the collar of her low-cut blouse.)

It seems to me sometimes wonderful how little I questioned the life of Cyril's parents, or even noticed much about them. I came once on his mother weeping, and stood awkwardly in the doorway as she wiped her tears and tried to laugh away the situation. "I'm just a silly woman," she said, "pay no attention. You won't mention it to Cyril, will you?"

I shook my head. The terrible pity and scorn I felt for her (not, notice, terror: it never occurred to me that I could end like her, and I did not) are palpable to me still. That first summer, unlike the later ones, which melted together in memory, seems to me to have the clarity still of one of those movies, popular when I was a young woman, where memory is created before our eyes as though we had returned there in a time machine, able to see it all.

"I had a little girl once, for a few hours," Cyril's mother said to me. "I would have liked to have a daughter. But we are lucky to have Cyril, and must not ask God for more." I think I knew that she wanted to take me in her arms, that if I had ruushed to her we would have embraced with a passion that would later have embarrassed us both. But I did not move; I stood, mute and powerless. She was lonely, of course; I understood that. Her husband dined in hall every night; when he took her to some rare occasion that included wives, she felt inadequate, felt she had failed him in some unspoken way. Did I know all that? Yes. But I blamed her for being a fool, forgave him for finding her a bore. One might have thought that, motherless, I would welcome this candidate for the position; the truth was, I had had enough of mothers — at any rate, enough of substitutes. Did I believe that one day I would awaken a boy, and take my place in the male world, treating women with the scorn they deserved, and, of course, the paternal kindness? Did my aunt not suggest this view was possible even to one who did not change gender?

Eventually, that afternoon, Cyril's mother returned to the kitchen, where she seemed always to be struggling with food or damp clothes, and I wandered out toward the Oxford Colleges, which I had taken as my special subject. I was fast becoming an authority on them. Cyril did not welcome me into his life every afternoon. That day, I walked to Wadham College, to the great copper beech, which is, I believe, still there: I sat beneath it in my schoolgirl outfit, and, as I had learned to do in that place, indulged in fantasies. An American couple accosted me.

"Do you know what college this is, little girl?" they asked.

I leapt to my feet, and got my English accent firmly into place. "Yes, sir," I said. "This is Wadham."

"Do you know the names of the others?" he asked.

"Arthur," his wife said.

"You wanted to see the University," he told her. "We might as well learn something.

Would you," he said, turning to me, "like to show us around Oxford? If, that is, you've nothing better to do?"

And so, as though some fantasy had materialized, some miracle quietly occurred, I led them through the colleges, telling them all the obvious things. Merton, Balliol, Trinity, All Souls — which I described from the outside; one was not allowed to enter. I knew only that there were no students, and no visitors, and that important men met there for profound, empire-shaking, discussions. I was on my way to Christ Church when the woman said her feet hurt, and the man said, "I guess we'll have to let it go at that. We've learned a lot, thanks to you." And he handed me two half crowns. A fortune, in those days, to an eight-year-old.

And thus began my career as a child Oxford guide. I borrowed, undetected, a small three-legged stool from the night nursery, and would sit where the tourists were likely to appear. I learned how, ingratiatingly, to offer my services. I made up a school to say I went to; my accent was impeccable, at least to foreign ears. I always wore my school uniform, even in the hot Oxford summer days, and learned to leap to my feet, and say "sir" and "ma'am" in every sentence. Part of my earnings, which I mostly stored away, I spent on a boy's school cap; the girl's hat that had been part of my uniform I thought soppy. I used to lift my cap, and put it back, as though I were a boy. It had an emblem on it, and I made up the name of the school to fit the cap.

I told Cyril nothing of this career, which I only practiced when he was off with his friends, having scorned me. To go with him or his group anywhere was worth anything to me: to be a boy, one of them. I would have given up any other opportunity for that. Yet I did not tell him of my service to tourists, though certainly it would have stood me in good stead with him and his friends. I know that I rationalized my failure to confide in him my newfound source of income and importance as a plan to spend the money on a gift for him; in reality, as I knew even then, had he offered himself to the tourists they would not have chosen me. Who would take a girl if they could get a boy?

Most of the time, however, Cyril and I were alone together through the long summer days of England. My aunt, when the Trinity term was over, had gone for a month to Europe. Cyril's father went to his college just the same, or perhaps to the library; we did not ask. He dined, even during the leave, in hall.

In the long evenings, when "we had to go to bed by day," as Robert Louis Stevenson wrote in one of the poems, Cyril's mother read to us. Our bedtime was made more bearable by *Alice in Wonderland* and other English stories and poems that I can still hear the voice of Cyril's mother intoning, gently, and with much expression. Because Cyril and I, catching one another's eye, could pretend that we listened for her sake, we could abandon ourselves to Leigh Hunt's Jenny, to A *Child's Garden of Verses*, to E. Nesbit's children; above all, to Alice.

In the day, when we were together, we never talked about what we had read, or about our elders. We raced about Oxford together, bareheaded (my cap was solely for business uses); on some afternoons, waiting by the boat-rental place in the hope that someone — for we were, Cyril especially, appealing children — would offer us a ride with them in a punt. On rare occasions my aunt, when she had returned from her vacation, took us on outings, to Blenheim, which we did not tell her we knew better than she; to the Cotswolds — the towns with the leaping trout and friendly pubs — and several times to London. For these occasions our uniforms were carefully pressed; we were given freshly ironed

73

shirts to wear, and were very well behaved.

I fear I have painted my aunt as rather stern and unbending. This was not always the case. She was one of those people, I think, who never claim to like children, and who therefore treat them with a certain distant respect that is returned. Children, I have noticed, are quick to observe where respect is not required. Where they recognize its rights, however, they are able to establish relationships with adults that combine formality and intimacy in a particularly appealing way. So it is, I like to think, with my relationship to Jean and Ted's children; so it was with my aunt and Cyril and me. I know that I won certain points with Cyril because she was my aunt, however honorary; he would not, without my presence, have had the trips, the ice creams. She treated us scrupulously alike, which I might have resented, were I another sort of child. Since, however, I accepted Cyril's superior claims as a boy, I was pleased enough to be treated on a par with him. And, needless to say, I adored being taken for an English child, even an English girl. My aunt liked my crisp, formal manners, and began, I sensed, to approve of me more as the summer went on. Perhaps it was during our outings that she was deciding whether or not to have me back to visit in future summers.

One day, toward the end of summer, my aunt asked me alone (that is without Cyril) to tea in her apartment. He ran off, pretending to join his friends, and I felt disloyal to him, going alone. But I had asked that he might come too, and she had told me firmly that she wished to talk with me, just the two of us. I had never before been to her apartment, which had its own entrance at the rear of the house, and occupied the top floor and an attic. She had gone to the trouble to buy an elegant cake for our tea, which she served at a table near the window overlooking the garden. I had thought I would be shy with her, but she was so direct, so unmanipulating, that I found myself able to address her directly, without dropping my eyes, my voice, or my tea.

"Would you like to come here every summer, and stay with Cyril and his parents, and have outings with me?" she asked. I said that I would, very much; that I loved England, adored Oxford, and would prefer, if asked, to live all year round here, and go to a real school with a real uniform.

"I'm afraid that's not possible," she said. "For one thing, during the winter Cyril is in school all day, and I am very busy indeed. Besides, your people in America would miss you."

"No they wouldn't," I said. "I'm sure they wouldn't."

"Your father would miss you," she said. "Think about it a minute. Surely you can see that."

"It would be easier for him if I weren't there," I said. "Then he could spend all his time with her." My aunt knew I meant his wife, who was nice enough to me — but I did not contribute in any way to the intimacy of their first years of marriage. I was willing, furthermore, to let her have my father, in exchange for Cyril and England.

"I think that is not quite fair to him," my aunt said.

"But I like England better than America. People behave better." Since my aunt certainly agreed with me, she found this argument difficult to counter.

"That," she said firmly, helping me to another piece of cake, "is not the question. I have not asked you where you want to live. I have asked you whether you would like to return next summer."

I nodded, afraid that I might cry. Among my fantasies under the copper beech at Wadham (and, indeed, everywhere else) had been that my aunt would tell me I could stay forever. Somehow, I cannot now imagine why, I thought it harder to turn into a boy in America. Probably it was the clothes; in the States at that time, girls wore very girlish clothes: blue jeans for both sexes were far off. Perhaps it was the manners I liked, or to show people around the colleges at Oxford; perhaps I found that the formal ways of English childhood distinguished less between the sexes.

"Never mind," my aunt said briskly, pleased, I guess now, that I wanted to stay, but fearing an outburst. "You have next summer to look forward to. Cyril's mother seems happy to have you back. She's a lonely woman, as you may have noticed. Well, that's settled anyway. There's only one other thing." I looked up at her. "I'm not, as you already know, your aunt. Neither your mother nor your father have any siblings. But I was a good friend of your mother's, and I shall serve well as an honorary aunt. We shall be honorary relations to each other, which is the best kind. In years to come, someone may suggest to you, it may occur to you, that I am really your mother. That's the sort of romantic story people like to dream up. Well, I'm not your mother. But I shall be as good a friend to you as I can, and I hope that will suffice. And, what is more, I will promise you this. If, when you are ready for University, you would like to go to one of the Oxford women's colleges — Somerville or Lady Margaret Hall — for preference, and are clever enough to get a scholarship, I shall see to it that you can go. Is it a bargain? You must, you see, work hard and get good grades, and prepare for the English entrance exam in time. I shouldn't think it would be hard to be a good student in America, and we shall be certain to pick up the slack if we have to."

The idea of Oxford, even a woman's college (and in the remaining days of my stay, I spent a good deal of time looking at them, particularly Somerville, where my aunt had been a student; women's colleges had never been part of my guided tour), came to fill my dreams, secretly, a pact with myself should I fail to become a boy. But, somehow, well before I was ready for University, I knew I would have to settle for an American college. The reasons were never stated; I suppose Oxford was too hard to arrange, or too expensive. There may have been other reasons to do with my aunt's health, or position. There were other summers with Cyril and my aunt — eventually Cyril's father found out about the guided tours, and shamed Cyril about not having thought of that and, Cyril's refusing to join me, I had to give them up if I was to keep his friendship — other trips to London, a time when we were allowed to go alone; a time when we were allowed to take a punt out by ourselves. But for me England is always that first year, when I was not unalterably committed to a girl's destiny, and had found a friend.

Five

WINIFRED'S JOURNAL

On the farm, each day was the same, varying only as Ted or Jean decided to assign me another afternoon task from four to seven, in place of the milking, which they then took on. I quite liked driving the tractor over the fields, with a corn chopper behind me, behind it the wagon to collect the silage. But that was only in the fall. In the summer, when not milking, I drove into the fields to cut grass for the cows, leaving it for them on large tables in the near fields. My tasks varied with the seasons, but not as much as Ted's and Jean's, for I had only the constant milking, or its substitute. They often worked far into the evenings in the summers; in the winters, they did the necessary repairs, and indoor jobs.

The sameness of my days, with only the change of seasons to mark time's passage, the hard work alternating with the reading, and writing, and pondering, were what I needed then: that I had been able not only to invent it for myself, but to bring it into being, seemed to me wonderful. How often we live wholly the prisoner of events we summoned, or did not summon, with no knowledge of what they would entail. I had made the life I now lived. There were minor, unforeseen surprises. Sometimes, oftener than I would have chosen, one of the children would be waiting for me outside the milking parlor, to be allowed to clean the cow's teats, and release her food into her milking place. Stanchions were no longer used; in the parlor the cows stood each in her place, eating, content to be milked by the machine I slung into place beneath each: the milking machines were too heavy for the children. The milk ran directly into the cooler, so it was, in fact, untouched by human hands, as they used to say, even before it was pasteurized — except for the fact that I would dip into it for the cats' milk, and Jean or Ted always took the milk for the house from the cooler. (I dislike milk, and only took some if I needed it for some unusual concoction.) None of us ever drank pasteurized milk, though Jean told me that when the babies were weaned, she bought milk in the store, the doctor having so advised. Occasionally, a cow would have to be stripped by hand; not often. The work became rhythmic, instinctive; and the children would talk to me about one thing and another, offering to help. Remembering my own childhood loneliness, I did not send them away. But I did not answer personal questions, and kept them at a certain distance.

One day a week, Jean, on her way to Pittsfield for one thing or another, would drop me off in Lenox, which had the best library in that area. I took out many books, the maximum allowed, each week, and brought them back the next. Waiting for Jean to return, I would begin to read in the library, rarely walking through the town, which in summer was terribly touristy, and in winter without major interest. But there was a bookstore I visited, having, in general, no money for books, but occasionally seeing a title I would determine to get from the library.

On one such bookstore visit, a month or so earlier, I had seen a biography of my aunt. I picked it up, already transported to another world. Had the bookstore exploded at that moment, I would not have noticed. There was the picture of her as Principal of her college on the cover. The biography was not authorized; indeed, the author had had no help with it at all, as she proudly announced, except for some old acquaintances, glad enough to say a few bitter words about my aunt. The book called her a snob, of course, and "revealed" that she had had an illegitimate child: me, I supposed. I had heard this rumor often, though few knew who the child was, or where she lived, or even, for certain, if she was a she. By now, the whole subject irritated me.

At this time there had been a trend in the world that I found deeply puzzling: the search, by adopted children, for their "real" parents. Some law, in England and America, opened the adoption records to these children, and they searched for their mothers with an assiduousness that, inevitably, found its way into novels I read from the Lenox library. It seemed to me a particularly female need, this finding of the "real" mother; what did it matter? I suspect the truth to be that women have so little adventure in their lives, after the days of "romance," or at the time of the failure of "romance," that they look for drama, not in future stories, as yet untold, but in the past story of their birth, the same old plot. It is not that I think the truth of their parentage should be kept from adopted children, but rather that this backward search, which makes good novels, makes bad living.

I think back, of course, but not to my parents: to Oxford, and those delicious summers. When I first came to work for Ted and Jean, and fell into a satisfactory way of life, I read all the books on Oxford I could find in the library. Most of them did not satisfy me at all; there were only two, in fact, that I relished, one by James Morris, who had lived near Oxford, and rendered it with a happy grace combined of experience and good writing. The other book, a collection of essays by those who had attended Oxford, intrigued me less, except that John Betjeman had gone to the Dragon School — so, to my astonishment, had Antonia Fraser (Cyril never mentioned girls in the school, and indeed, had he, my universe would have whirled about my head); Betjeman's description recalled Cyril and his talk of school through all those golden summers.

James Morris relates best the inevitable recollections of Oxford weather, as opposed to the real weather. (Is real weather, to be discovered by diligent research, as important as "real" parents?) "The meteorological records for those parts," Morris wrote, and I copied out, "assure us that July 4, 1862, was 'cool and rather wet'; but on that day Lewis Carroll first told the tale of *Alice in Wonderland* to four people in a Thames gig, rowing upstream for a picnic tea, and to the ends of their lives all four remembered the afternoon as a dream of cloudless English sunshine." Morris reports that Oxford weather is the foulest to be found in England, yet "summer is more summery here than anywhere else I know; not hotter, certainly not sunnier, but more like summers used to be, in everyone's childhood memories." So I was not alone in remembering that. If it was nostalgia, it was a universal nostalgia, somehow less threatening to one's sense of reality. I knew as a child, of course, loitering beneath the copper beech in the Wadham gardens, that one summer term a great cedar tree there had been killed by a snowstorm. I knew too that Cyril and I, each equipped with a blanket and stern instructions about coming directly home, were allowed to go to outdoor night performances of Shakespeare, and that almost always (it seems now) we watched in the rain, making it a part of honor to stay until the end as the audience, ever more cowardly, or damp, thinned out.

Were all the summers the same? I know that the farm children here will remember all the summers as the same, with only special events to mark different "times." Perhaps that is why in childhood it is always summer.

"Did you ever milk cows when you were a little girl?" Pamela asked one day. I simply shook my head. Could I answer her that I had never been a little girl, but a chrysalis waiting to become the boy for which destiny had designed me? Pamela, the older, does everything her brother does, and Jean is as reliable as Ted on the farm. Had I grown up at such a time, in such a way, what should I have become?

I had bought the biography of my aunt, terrible as it obviously was. I rationalized the spending of the money, as I had done even as a child, by calling it a birthday present. The falseness of the whole book astonished me; it was a picture of my aunt drawn by one who had hated or envied her, someone (I suspected) who, secretly admiring her, wrote the book to defeat that admiration. My aunt, who was the author of novels that sold very well and as a formidable scholar and the Principal of an Oxford college, incurred the particular wrath of many influential English intellectuals at the universities after the war. The lengths they went to to jeer at her in books and journal articles were indeed a compliment, as I know she considered it. But they did provide, in future years, permission to treat her with more rudeness than is usually accorded Oxbridge people, however irritating. Had her friends authorized a biography in the first place, they might have avoided all this; now they could hardly complain of outrageous suppositions, when they had refused the very papers that would have made those suppositions impossible.

Reading over what I have lately written, I see that I refer to "my mother and father." Oddly, I always thought of them as that, I suppose because "mothers and fathers" to me meant those who, male and female, ran the home you returned to each day, and had control over your life until you were old enough to leave. I know that my father loved me, and my stepmother, as much as I would have liked, being a reading child, to cast her in the role of cruel usurper of my rights, was a reasonable woman dealing with a situation in which she was determined to do her best. She loved my father — he was, indeed, as I early sensed, a man of powerful attraction to women — and she readily accepted the condition that I came with him, if he married, and love for me was included in love for him. She would certainly have found a conventional child easier to deal with: I refused all her ministrations as to dress and behavior but not, oddly, as to decorum. I sensed, and my summers with Cyril and the manners of English boys reinforced this, that a kind of rigid courtesy protected one's thoughts and opinions from too close scrutiny. I think children lost a good deal when the mores in America denied them a certain rigidity of manner, for their sakes alone. Acting out one's aggressions, impressing one's peers with one's rudeness, is enervating, and dilutes the central self's coherence.

I now understand that the summer arrangement, by which, from the age of eight on, I visited my aunt and boarded with Cyril's parents, came about through my stepmother's desire to have her "own" family for the summer; relating to me must have modified alarmingly her relations with my father, and the two children they subsequently had together. These, both girls (how clearly I sensed my stepmother's disappointment), I treated with a disdain that I considered highly correct, but which my stepmother must have found intolerable; she tolerated it, nonetheless. (I notice here that I refer to her as my "stepmother," but I called her "mother" all those years, and thought of her as my "mother." Can it be that, like the adopted children looking for their birth-mother, I am making a distinction I scorn?)

Of course, I asked my mother, as I must call her, why I was being sent to England. "To visit your aunt," she said. "Is she my father's sister?" I asked. No, she is the sister of my dead mother. I think my stepmother believed this, although later, when my aunt told me, quite casually and flatly, that my mother was an only child, I did not bother mentioning this to anyone. I knew my aunt was not my "real" aunt; I concluded that she was the dear friend of my dead mother, that she had enacted, with my mother, a rare bond of female friendship that was not chatter about households and cooking and children, and that she wished to keep in touch with me, all that was left of that friendship. Was I told this, allowed to assume it, or did I make it up? I do not know, but, in later years, my aunt would talk of my mother in a way I hoped that some woman might, someday, speak of me. I see the contradiction here: while Cyril was my friend, while I intended to become a boy at that moment when I might turn into a woman, still, I dreamed of a woman friend.

If it is always summer in our memories of childhood, as many claim, perhaps that is why I never think of my home in those years, but only of Oxford, and can scarcely remember the Ohio city in whose suburbs I grew up. At this very moment, dropped into Oxford, I could find my way to the Shelley Memorial, and even (though I am now too large) know how to squeeze past the bars to stand behind the memorial itself, gazing at the plump buttocks of the reclining statue (did I realize that he was dead, that the muse supporting him was mourning?), which proved, Cyril assured me, that a girl had modeled the figure of Shelley. I know the underground passageways, and how to get into the colleges without being spotted by the ubiquitous porters, at least for a while. Of the Ohio city I remember nothing, nor would such memory serve, since the center of the city has been leveled, and shopping centers have taken over the mercantile life. Freudians would say, no doubt, that I have repressed that childhood. Argument is futile, but I have not repressed it; I have dismissed it, recalling clearly only one or two people. Except for them, I was never a part of it, but had my being elsewhere, at Oxford in the summers, in my fantasies before that.

And of the years before I was eight, before the Oxford summers? I know that I spent my earliest years in England, in a country cottage in Devon. I can remember the ocean, and the daffodils, and the woman who cared for me: she and I would ride in a pony cart into town once a week; we shopped together, going, as one does in England, to a different shop for each item — bread here, butter there. One day she told me (can I remember this? I was perhaps five) that my father was coming to take me home to America. Had I ever seen him before? I remember waiting for him by the gate, watching him descend from the car that brought him. (In later years, when I read *Adam Bede*, it seemed to me that the way Adam's mother waited for him to appear on the horizon was how I waited for my father that day; I disliked the connection, not wishing to be a woman who waited for a man to rescue her from meaninglessness.) We took a ship, my father and I, back to where I cannot remember; my stepmother told me that she had met my father in Boston, and that he had me with him then, but I never believed my stepmother. It was not that she lied; I never thought that. It was that I did not believe her to have access to the truth about most matters. Now, of course, I assume her accuracy in this.

The man and woman in search of me did not come back; they wrote me a letter. Ted left it for me to find when I went into the barn for the afternoon milking. (I got few letters, and had declined Ted's offer of my own mailbox. The local postman knew where I was, and left my mail in with Ted's. There was little enough of it: my quarterly check, an occasional bill.) This letter had been sent to Winifred Ashby, care of Ted Wilkowski. I put it into my back pocket, and went on with the milking. It was a day when I was alone with the cows, and I thought of earlier times, for which I did not usually yearn, when one milked by hand, and rested one's head against the cow's warm flank. There was not a cow in the herd now who would let you milk her by hand, though, because I had developed the habit of taking stale bread out to the fields for the heifers and the cows who were freshening, they knew me and were not skittish in my presence.

I went into the woods behind my house to read the letter; there was scarcely light enough, but I wanted the first shock of it to hit me outdoors, so that my house might remain a place of peaceful refuge. The idea of reviving memories of my aunt and Oxford excited and frightened me — frightened me because I had made my life into what I wanted it to be, and did not want to chase my thoughts through the past; I wanted to create my present. The letter, even when I had grasped that it was about my aunt, was unexpected:

Dear Miss Ashby:

We have been asked by Harriet St. John Merriweather to meet you personally, and to hand you a letter from her to you. Since you seem rather elusive, and our visit to the farm where you work [so they had established that] did not suggest your readiness to meet us, we are writing to ask if we might arrange a meeting with you. Miss Harriet St. John Merriweather, who was a friend of your aunt, Miss Charlotte Stanton, is eighty years old, and is therefore naturally interested in expediting her business with you. We suggest that you meet with us at the Red Lion Inn in Stockbridge on Wednesday at 7:00 o'clock, for dinner. Will you please telephone the number given below to let us know if you are willing to do so? We urge you to meet with us, and add, in encouragement, the old saw that if you get in touch with us you will learn something to your advantage.

The letter was signed by two names, and the telephone number given. My main problem, which I could hardly tell the signers, was the question of how I might get to Stockbridge. I decided, before returning from the woods, that I would ask Ted and Jean if I could borrow their car; it was against my principles, but these, after all, must bend to strange events. The telephone call was no problem: there is no charge for local calls, and there's an extension of the telephone in the barn. I would call tomorrow after the morning milking.

I walked directly to the house, and asked my favor, assuring Ted and Jean that it would not be a habit. I explained that it was important business from England.

"Connected to those two nosing around here the other day?" Ted asked.

"The same people," I said. "It has to do with an aunt of mine who died a while ago." That, not quite true, seemed to me a fair explanation; certainly I owed them one for borrowing their car.

"Maybe you'll be left a fortune, and give up milking," Jean said, I thought with regret.

"There were no fortunes to leave," I said. My aunt's inheritance was the royalties of her popular novels, and these had not come to me.

"I'm sorry about borrowing the car," I said as I left. "Please don't think of it as the thin edge of the wedge; I appreciate my position here, and shall try not to take advantage of it."

"You worry too much," Jean said, smiling at me. "If it will make you feel any better, you can pick up some food for the geese from the Agway on Route 7; they stay open till nine."

"I'll do that, and thanks," I said, smiling. Jean and I understood one another.

"I'll only go after the milking, which I'll start a little early on Wednesday," I said. "I'll tell them eight o'clock; they'll have to settle for that."

And next morning I left the message that I would meet them in the Red Lion Inn at eight Wednesday evening. Then I tried to put the matter out of my mind.

Six

Dearest Toby:

We have met her, enticed her, as I told George we would, by honesty and directness. His ridiculous assault on the farm had, of course, less than no results — what would anyone have thought? George, need I say, pictured her as some shrinking English spinster who would offer us parsnip wine once we had fluttered her maiden heart. How he reconciled this picture with a woman working as a farmhand, only George could say, if it even occurred to him. "She's an independent woman, George," said I, "with no more need of your attentions than of nettle rash. Ask her in a businesslike way, invite her to dinner, and probably she'll come out of normal human curiosity, or loyalty to her aunt or to old Harriet Sinjin," as I have taken to calling her. And I was right, as usual (I see you grin and bear it). She found us in

96

the dining room of the Red Lion Inn, which is touristy to a fare-thee-well, but does have a sort of garden restaurant where not being dressed to the nines doesn't stand out like a sore thumb.

She would have been noticeable in any case because she is tall, and carries herself with an air of confidence that I guess must have cost her years of effort: to make her body, I mean, into someplace she felt at home. I suspect it was the hard, physical work did it — have you ever noticed how women athletes move? No, my darling Toby, I'm sure you haven't given them a moment's thought. She was wearing long corduroy trousers with a tailored shirt and a smart ascot at the throat. We knew her at once, and I waved to her. George rather gaped, the fool: God knows what he expected.

She shook hands, sat down, and said to me: "You don't look as though you would be frightened by a goose." And she smiled; she has a lovely smile, which transforms her face from a rather sad mask, though not unhandsome, to a center of light. What nonsense I write you. I knew at once what she meant, though George, who was trying to offer her a drink, began to consider that perhaps she didn't need one. "I wasn't frightened," I said. "Just being a nuisance. I like the arrogance of geese, and I tempt them into thinking I'm a fool; naturally, they think any hu-

man who holds out a hand is a goose, as we would say." Oh Toby, why couldn't it be you in this with me, and not dreary George, I write for the thousandth time.

She and I liked each other at once, that's the glorious part. How shall I drown George? He will clearly muck the whole thing up if I can't shake him off. Why Harriet Sinjin should have had such a dreary son, only the mysterious ways of genes can say. He and I, however, had determined to do no more that evening than arrange a further meeting; my nefarious plan is to dump George into a ditch on the way to it. So we chatted a bit, though it was clear she liked chatter no more than I. I told her about myself; it seemed the kindest thing. George started off once or twice about his mama and her aunt, but I kicked him hard under the table.

"You have the same name as my aunt," she said, smiling.

"Yes," I said. "But I am always called Charlie and she was always Charlotte, never a diminutive, never Lottie, am I right?"

"Absolutely. Mostly, she was The Principal, or whatever title she had before that. She never tolerated informality and, as you must know if you know anything about her, thought most girls fools. She was convinced they turned away with astonishing resolution from the chances life of-

fered them. Perhaps they did."

And that, dear Toby, was her longest speech. She drank only iced tea, saying she had to drive. I feared I had met that most horrible of all social creatures, the adamant teetotaler, but she reassured me. "I've seen so many accidents from drunken driving around here," she said. "And it's a borrowed car." I had a bit the sense that she didn't want to introduce too great a note of conviviality just at first. She did ask about the letter from Sinjin. George handed it to her, as we had agreed. More later. (I see you reading this, sipping your drink at the end of the day and, I trust, missing me.) You are an angel, my angel, not to fuss about my coming away. I know how much you like my being there. But it was Stanton who brought us together, we must remember that, my love.

Dearest Toby:

We have met again, without George, who fnally saw that I was likely to make more progress alone. Poor George is one of those people for whom one can, in their absence, develop immense tolerance, and then dislike them intensely the moment one again claps eyes on them. He is such a pompous, damp, foolish mess. How Harriet Sinjin could have produced him — but I feel I have said that many times before. Our Winifred would

99

be a much more logical offspring. But of whom? That is the question.

The letter was short enough, in all conscience. But hadn't you or George read it? I hear you asking. No. We retained our purity, and left the seal intact. Probably because there were two of us. And whatever one might think of George, he is not the sort to steam open envelopes — even if he could figure out how. Anyway: it wouldn't be considered the pukka thing to do. If the suspense is killing you, I can offer no relief. Our Winifred didn't show me the letter. But she did sum up its contents, so she said, before putting it, with a final gesture, in her hip pocket. "It asks George to find me," she said, "if possible with Charlie's help — with your help," she added, smiling. "She hopes you both will succeed before she dies, an event she feels certain will take place as soon as she has finished her work on the Tudor manuscripts. If you succeeded, she asks to see me. She says that George will suffer if I do not come, since she cannot make out her will until then. Money for the trip to England will be provided. There's a bit more, but that's the substance."

When she had put the letter away, and got on with the milking process — have I mentioned that we were in the barn, and that the process begins by her opening a trapdoor and allowing bales of hay to fall at our feet (if we have remembered to move) that she then moves with a pitchfork to where the cows will stand? — she told me that she would have to think about it. For one thing, she did not wish to leave her employers in the lurch. I assured her that the trip could be done in a week, and that Sinjin's final manuscript had gone in; she awaited only the galleys. There was not all that much time, and the dear lady was, I reminded Winifred, about eighty bloody years old, and body and soul only held together by her need to see the last of the books through the press.

"Where do you come into all this?" she, of course, asked. It seemed to me characteristic of her not to have asked sooner. She is rather like a Henry James character, moving in a moral universe no one but she inhabits, but which she insists upon regarding as intact. To have asked the question sooner would have been rude, you see. And even now she bent over the machine that was milking the cow so that she might not appear to be watching me as I answered. I do like her, Toby, which is a help.

Dearest Toby:

She has agreed to go, having told the whole story to her farmers, and they understanding perfectly and appreciating her thoughtfulness. They were happy to get on without her for a week (which I can well imagine; I haven't met them, *except the male half, that once, but I'm sure they'd do a lot more than that to keep her. There can't be another creature in the world of either gender and sound mind who would want that job at that pay). But I said none of this to our Winifred, just told her I would get the tickets and arrange for us to fly together. George will have gone earlier, my dear, I having convinced him in my madly clever way that he should go ahead to be with Mama when we two turned up. My motive, of course, is to keep him away from Winifred, but it worked beautifully; I could see him hoping to consolidate himself with Sinjin prior to this new female influence upon her and his inheritance. Really, George is too much, and yet I can't really dislike the poor lamb, he's such a bumbling, self-satisfied fool. We fly on Monday night; Winifred is driving with me to Bradley airfield — it is nearer here, and I don't want to try to get in and out of New York, which will be complicated with hotels and taxis and such; I dread her faltering at the first opportunity. So I shall simply scoop her up on the farm in the afternoon (she will have to miss the milking, but I pointed out that she will be back for the evening milking that day week, so it all evens out — what a creature of honor she is) and we'll arrive at the airport in an hour and a half ready to fly off; no chance for slippage. I shan't have time to say* good-bye in person, my darling, which I much regret, but you do understand the urgency. I intend to hover over her like a guardian angel for the remaining days.

Dearest Toby:

There has not been a moment to write, though I hoped to scrawl this letter in moments at Sinjin's house as I waited outside for the great interview. I only hope you can read it; I doubt your work has accustomed you to outrageous handwriting; we poor biographers must get used to it. (How is everything at Dar and Dar going? I do think of it often, in between our dramatic moments.)

Well, my dear, we arrived at dawn, as usual on these damn flights, and made our weary way through customs, immigration, etc. (I forgot to tell you, of course, that our Winifred's passport, which I only thought of at the last possible moment, if you can believe it, turned out to be quite all right. I suspect her of leaving herself always the opportunity to fly back to England when the fancy took her. A good sign, I think.) Once we had cleared all the Heathrow hurdles, we took the bus to London, dumped our bags at the hotel, and went by underground to Ladbroke Grove, where Sinjin lives. I didn't quite know how to prepare our Winifred for the meeting, except to say that the house was a bit of a rat's nest: it was *the home, I said, of someone who thought of nothing but Elizabeth I's England, in all its detail, and, I suspected, lived there herself most of the time. I thought of describing Sinjin, but in the end decided not to. With anyone else, I would have gone out of my way to suggest, ever so delicately, that Sinjin in no way resembled the old ladies in films and BBC productions: neatly coiffed white hair, and lean, bony faces full of character. But Winifred, I felt certain, given her own obvious unconventionality, would not even notice if she met a woman who couldn't have cared less what she looked like, as long as her work was sound. I thought I would just leave it to them to get on or not: maturity, my dear, in case you hadn't noticed, is letting things happen.*

Have I described Sinjin to you? It suddenly occurs to me that you may not know quite what I mean. You know she is eighty, more or less, and mumbles about herself as the ancient of days. Stairs are difficult, though she lives, like all the English with their proud devotion to discomfort, in a narrow three-story attached house. She walks with a stick, and complains about her memory, which seems damn good to me, if rather limited to Tudor times and the further reaches of her own life. She answers slews of letters every day, partly from people wanting to know about Winifred's aunt, what with all her books still be-

ing in print, and as far as I can see functions rather better than most of what are now called the old-old. The point, however, is that she is fat, with great dewlaps of flesh, and next to no hair on her head: what is there is white. "Wispy" is the best one could say for it. She has great fat legs that I'm certain impede her already difficult progress. Ninety-nine people out of a hundred would snicker, but ninety-nine people wouldn't give a damn for the Tudors or know what they were in the presence of. I trusted that Winifred would.

It wasn't a bit clear, when Winifred emerged and we left after the first visit, how it had all gone. (She went alone the next time, riding the underground like a native, but of course I keep forgetting that England is familiar ground to her, at least its geography: she did exclaim at the number of Arab women in the streets with little leather hoods on their noses.) Our Winifred is not one of your talky types. But she did mention how much she liked Sinjin, how much she admired her — "like my aunt, always saying it's the work you do that matters" — so I am full of hope. George has been banished to his club, where it is supposed that he plays bridge all day, and prays, while dummy, that all will be well. He is even muttering about golf, so I am fairly sure we've got him off our hands.

Dearest Toby:

Sorry for all the time that has passed, but your marvelous call last night makes me feel better. Bless you, dear man, for thinking of it. It was heaven to hear your voice. By the time you get this I'll have the final big news about the biography.

Winifred and Sinjin talked, my dear, by the hour; I think Sinjin quite forgot the Tudors. "And what did you talk about?" asked I of Winifred. "Oh, her childhood — did you know she wanted to be a boy in a cap and a striped blazer? — and her meeting with my aunt, and the years at Oxford, and the times afterward, and their friendship and her marriage, Sinjin's I mean, and George."

"A wonderful list of topics," I said, with my usual mild irony, "but what exactly did you say about them; how did the discourse go? You know, and I said, and she said, and she said they said . . ." But our Winifred only smiled and said that she couldn't talk about it yet, not that it was a secret, just that she didn't want to talk about it till she'd digested it. And with that, of course, I had to be content, particularly as she was (and is) consideration itself. Which is to say, I may have missed the delicious tidbits, the memories, the scandal — which by now I am sniffing at every turn — but she has been frank enough about the decisions the two of them reached, cackling at the

top of that narrow house, Sinjin's fat legs and Winifred's long ones stretched out, no doubt, toward the inadequate electric heater.

"What you'll want to know about," our Winifred said, "is what she has decided about the biography of my aunt, the papers, all that. She hasn't terribly much confidence in George, but she was willing to leave it all to him, if I turned out to be a disappointment, or uninterested in her or my aunt. Once she saw I was interested, and wasn't particularly disappointing, she said she would leave it up to me what was to happen to the papers, to the biography, to the lot. It seems her will, which was made in the States (I could hardly shout: 'I know, by my lover'), is still OK. I'll have control over all her papers, etc. She asked if I thought you would be a good biographer of my aunt, and I said yes, I thought you would be. So I don't think there should be any problem about that. George and I are to split the proceeds from my aunt's books; she offered it all to me, but I said no, I'd turned up only at the last moment and that was hardly fair to George. And, of course, all proceeds of the biography will be yours."

Well, Toby my sweet, one couldn't ask fairer than that. She told me she'd grown to like and respect me, and thought I would do a good biography — anyway, there was no reason she could see

107

why I wouldn't. "But will you cooperate?" *I asked. She said she couldn't honestly say how much she would tell me of matters to do with herself, but most of it would be evident in the papers, anyway, and she didn't intend to withhold anything.*

"Did you happen to ask," I couldn't keep myself from saying, "how Sinjin came to have a son like George? Bridge, golf, and but a smattering of brain?" "I didn't ask, but she told me." Winifred looked down at her hands, and after a pause that seemed to demand my saying something out of sheer decency, she went on: "Sinjin's father was a charming man, quite smart, but he'd inherited some money and he did nothing but play golf and bridge. He thought them the two most delightful things in the world, certainly far superior to little Harriet and her mother. When little Harriet grew up she despaired of intellectual men, and saw no point in upper-class men like her father, who only amused themselves, so she married a garage mechanic." "A garage mechanic!" *I screamed. We were sitting in St. James's Park, but I think they heard me in the Channel Islands. Winifred, of course, looked around like a startled doe, and I cursed myself for an idiot. But she did smile.* "What Sinjin said, is: 'Unfortunately George inherited his grandfather's frivolous interests but not his brain; his fa-*

ther's mindlessness but not his craft; and my figure." But, Winifred went on to tell me, all Sinjin
really wanted for George, now that Winifred was
found, was as much income as she could leave
him, plus her house, which to judge from the real-
estate agents who called every week, had risen
marvelously in value. ("They'll have to put in another loo," I nastily added.) "The point was,"
Winifred said, "Sinjin didn't know what to do
with my aunt's stuff, and she wanted to leave the
royalties, which are still handsome, to me. But I
persuaded her to leave all that to George too; we
finally compromised on splitting it."

"I don't know why you should be so generous,"
I said, "if you don't mind my speaking bluntly.
You can't go on milking cows all your life."

"I already have a small income," Winifred
said. "I do think it's George's by right. After all,
he might very well not have found me." "He'd
certainly not have found you," I said, "which is
why Sinjin sent me along, knowing my motive
besides. I think you owe it to me to take the
money." "I'm taking half," Winifred said, and I
couldn't get another word out of her.

Tomorrow we are both to meet with Sinjin. I
was rather surprised when Winifred told me, but
pleased, as you can imagine. I expect to be lec-
tured about being nice to George, and the respon-
sibilities of a biographer, which I shall take with

even more than my usual good grace since I am so fond of the plucky old bag. Winifred clearly thinks Sinjin is some sort of miracle, dropped into Winifred's path like manna for the Hebrews. I can't think why; it isn't as though Winifred were writing a biography. Don't think (I know you won't fail to think, you beast) that such a fear didn't grasp me by the very entrails. But Winifred seemed to sense all this, and has reassured me that writing a biography of her aunt is the very last thing she would ever want to do, next to being a bridesmaid. She has even burst forth from time to time, as this will evidence, with a quip. I rather think that our Winifred detests the whole question of clothes and what to wear, and may have been drawn to Sinjin, who, God knows, gives the matter no thought whatever, because of this. Even a dowdy old woman can be a respected scholar — that sort of thing.

After Sinjin, Oxford, I think, for a day or two. Winifred has agreed to show me some of the spots in her childhood, in London and in Oxford, where she and aunty set forth upon the world. I think already, my love, of returning to you soon. I do hope you'll call again, before you get this, to start my day in the right frame of mind, because . . .

Seven

The private detective who came to see Kate, after she had finished reading the documents given her by Charlie, was calm, businesslike, and so little resembling any American novelist's idea of a private detective that Kate wondered, for several moments, whether he was an impostor sent as a joke by Toby and Charlie. Such, she thought, are the impositions of fictions upon our minds. She had invited him home to tea, serving this from a set bequeathed her, as the only daughter, by her mother. Kate's housekeeper, who entered into the spirit of things with a remarkable verve, especially when she sensed the revival of the manners of an earlier era, had made watercress sandwiches and thin, elegant cookies. Kate, asking him if he wanted cream or lemon, felt transported back into an English detective story of the twenties. The detective, whose name was appropriately Mr. Fothingale, but who asked to be called Richard, requested lemon and sugar and settled down to his longish tale of frustration and few results. Kate, sipping tea with lemon and no sugar, and relishing the delicate watercress sandwiches, urged him on with smiles and nods of appreciation.

"I began," he said, "with what you've seen in those documents. Minus the Ashby journal, of course. I found that after I began on the job. It was just about all I did find. After the last letter of Charlie's you have there, Winifred Ashby disappeared and hasn't been heard from since. By anyone."

"Was the journal in her A-frame house on the farm?" Kate asked.

"It was; locked away in the drawer of a table she used for writing. I honestly don't think she'd have left it there if she didn't intend to come back, and as far as I was concerned that was the best evidence we had that she hadn't done a bunker. Of course," he said, holding up an admonishing hand as Kate started to speak, "it's always possible she left it there to mislead us. She was such a private person that I did wonder if she wouldn't have been more likely to have taken it with her.

But she was only going for a week. I think she trusted the farmers enough not to riffle through her things, and she did take the precaution of putting a strong lock on the table drawer. I mean, someone would have really had to jimmy it to get at her stuff, as we finally did."

"I wonder," Kate said. "If she were really secretive, as I used to be, wouldn't she have hidden it somewhere unlikely, where it would never be found?"

"I thought of that too. But I don't know if you've ever seen an A-frame from the inside. There just aren't that many hiding places — it's not like an old house with paneling and nooks and crannies. And there is no storage space whatever, to tuck something away in the back of. She could have put it in the refrigerator, or the stove, or in some other piece of furniture, or she could have hidden it in the barn — but that wasn't really her territory. No, in the end, I think she did the safest thing, always supposing she was intending to come back." Kate nodded.

"And, after all," he went on, "what did that bit of journal tell us? A lot about her childhood in Oxford, and how she came to work at the farm, but nothing you could go on. I mean, the fact that she would have liked to have been a boy doesn't really lead anywhere when you really think about it, does it? Except, of course, if she decided she'd wanted it so long she'd try, and turned herself into a man — you know, passing herself off as one. That could be rather hard to trace."

"I doubt it," Kate said. "For what my opinion's worth, and at this stage that's not much, I doubt it. She had wanted to be a boy — what girl of spirit hasn't? Both the women scholars Charlie writes to Toby about wanted to be boys. But that's a long way from disguising yourself as a man for any length of time. Particularly these days, when women can dress with all the comfort to be found in men's clothes, if they want to."

"One of the many leads I followed," Richard said, holding out his cup for more tea, "was that she'd taken another job as a farmhand. Mind you, I didn't believe it for a minute. But that was because I believed what she said in her journal, which could have been a trap to lead me to exactly that conclusion. So I did a lot of investigating about farmhands recently hired in the area, and even out into other parts of New England. It's easy to say in a sentence, isn't it, but it took a long time, asking the questions, paying the tokens of appreciation, waiting for news to trickle back.

Fortunately, most farmers love to gossip, men and women both. Theirs is a lonely life, so why shouldn't they? The upshot was, the new hands, recently hired, all turned out to be too short, or too fat, or with a beard, or definitely not Winifred Ashby. Disguise will go only so far. And for what it's worth, the farmers she was working for didn't believe she'd run out on them, any more than Charlie did. Winifred Ashby may have been the world's greatest con artist, but if you're that talented, why waste it all on some farmers and a woman biographer who's going to go ahead with her biography anyway? I mean, whom was she conning, and why? For what?"

"The answer does seem to lie in England, with the two women scholars, Charlotte and Sinjin, doesn't it?"

"That certainly seems clear. I spent a lot of time in England, and a lot of money — Charlie's money. I don't come cheap, and there were fares, et cetera. What I'm here to tell you is that I found out nothing; that is, everything I found out was negative. Charlie said I could charge her for this talk with you, but I won't. I hope you can see something I haven't seen. It probably will turn out that the farmers murdered her for some nest egg we don't even know about, buried the body on their farm, and left her journal because it led to a false trail. I just don't believe it."

"Isn't there some record of her return to this country by airplane?"

"Not really. One of the airlines did cough up, after what nudging on my part I can barely describe, the fact that a passenger listed as Winifred Ashby flew back to the U.S. right after she disappeared in England. But that proves nothing. Anyone can say they're Winifred Ashby. Don't say it, I know what you're going to ask: What about her passport? The airlines are not that careful about checking passports against tickets, and anyway, handing them a different passport than one's own, supposing someone else were traveling as Winifred Ashby, wouldn't be hard. The U.S. has no record of her entering or leaving the country, and wouldn't give it to me if they had. There would be a record on her passport, of course, but that disappeared with her. I hope you begin to see the dimensions of the problem."

Kate smiled at Mr. Fothingale. She admired him, not only because he was frustrated beyond the call of duty, but because he was willing to turn all he had learned over to her, which was an act of true generosity. She was not a competitor exactly. She took no fees for her investigations — indeed, they usually ended up costing her money. Nobody poor can be an amateur detective for long. Yet, despite all this to Mr. Fothingale's credit, Kate was troubled by a doubt. She decided to state it, not without considerable trepidation.

"Please don't let this question offend you," she said. "No, that's not the honest way to put it. Please realize that I have to ask it, and that no doubt of your probity inspires it." Richard Fothingale nodded. "Can I be certain," Kate asked, "that you aren't giving me the case now because you suspect, or guess, that Charlie herself or Toby Van Dyne is involved in Winifred Ashby's disappearance? Please don't misunderstand," Kate added nervously.

Richard put his cup down on the table. "If you hadn't asked that," he said, "I'd have thought you a fool. The plot you mention crossed my mind very early in the investigation. Coming to me that way had to be the cleverest ploy possible, if Charlie had done away with Winifred. I can't prove she didn't, or that Mr. Van Dyne didn't. I don't believe they're other than they seem, and I didn't give the case over to you because I feared my clients were guilty. That's the truth, but if I were you, I'd check it out."

"The point seems to be that nothing checks

out. What about Cyril, for instance?"

"I'm afraid that's clear enough; Cyril died before he was thirty, though I have to admit the thought of his having taken someone else's identity and come back for some reason was exciting — not that I could imagine what the reason would be, or how it would affect Winifred. It's not even clear how much time, if any, they spent together as young adults."

"Reading her journal," Kate said, "I seem to think of her only as a child, dressed in her school outfit, showing Americans around Oxford. She seems to be an eternal child, like Alice and the children in the Nesbit books."

"Charlie said you would get literary. I stick to records. The records are very clear on Cyril. He died of Hodgkin's disease. Probably he thought of his childhood and Winifred when he knew he was dying. We know he remembered her, and with great affection, because he made her his beneficiary after his mother's death. His mother, poor woman, outlived him but she's dead now."

"She seemed to have outlived her life even when the children were young."

"Yes," Richard said. "She was a sad one, wasn't she?"

"And Winifred knew it, then and when she wrote the journal. But where does that get us?"

"Well," Richard went on, a bit more briskly, "there are plenty of details. Of Cyril's life, and Charlotte Stanton's life, and even a bit on Harriet St. John Merriweather, Sinjin. Now, there's an amazing old bag, if you don't object to the expression. She was perfectly clear about what she'd said to Winifred, and what was to be in her will, and who was to be literary executor, and all the rest of it."

"Did you meet her?" Kate asked."

"Oh, yes. She died only a short time ago. I met George too."

"An inspiring experience, I'm to gather." Kate smiled at him.

"I had trouble at first believing he was real. His conversation filled with 'don't you knows' and 'well, never minds' and, something else he kept saying: 'I haven't a clue.' He hadn't, either, if you ask me."

"Could it have possibly been an act?" Kate asked.

"Didn't I hope so! That's the trouble with this case. You keep smelling a rat, thinking, This is just too good to be true, and then finding out it is true. I followed every lead there is, short of reading the books of both those lady authors. Maybe you'll find something there. That's the hope, I daresay, in their engaging a literary specialist."

"I doubt it, really," Kate said. "Charlie has read all the books. I think what they want is a fresh mind, and one that doesn't charge too much, or make them feel too foolish. After all, if someone as thorough and knowledgeable as you failed, where else can they go?"

"To a lady professor, of course," Richard said. "Do you mind if I finish up the cookies? They're fine."

"Do," Kate said. "And I shall finish the watercress sandwiches. More tea?" Richard nodded. "Let's go over it again, if you don't mind," Kate said. "I'll try not to be too tedious. Everything in Winifred's journal checks out; you've seen to that. What about the Ohio people, by the way?"

"That's clear enough. Winifred's school records are still there, and records of the house the family owned. The father's dead, but the mother and the two other daughters were easily discovered. I went to see them."

"You *have* been thorough. Nothing there, I'm to assume."

"Nothing of great interest, though you might see it differently. Winifred left home at eighteen, and never returned. She kept decently in touch; the sisters spoke of her with what I would call modified affection — closer to awe, really. The mother just said she'd

120

never succeeded with Winifred, hard as she had tried. I believe her. Winifred sent Christmas cards, and responded to announcements of marriages, births, that sort of thing. She was polite but uninterested. No motive anywhere that I could see."

"What about money? Always a motive where there's money."

"When the father died he left his estate to his wife, in trust, with a third to each of his daughters on her death. When she dies, that's how it will be. Perhaps the other two would gang up to kill Winifred for a third of a hundred thousand dollars in the future, but I don't see it that way."

"It would be hard to," Kate admitted.

Richard put his cup down with a certain note of finality. "I guess that about covers it," he said, "unless you can think of something else. I don't mean to rush you."

"When did Winifred disappear, exactly?" Kate asked. "Charlie's letters stop as they were about to visit Sinjin. Did they visit her, in fact?"

"Sorry. I thought you knew all about that. Often happens in cases, I've noticed. Everyone assumes everyone else knows something terribly obvious, and when it's clear they don't, bob's your uncle (I picked that up from George, too)."

"It's a neat trick in detective stories," Kate added. "My favorite is one book in which the cast consists of musicians, mostly amateur but a few professionals, including a famous conductor, and no one gets around to telling the detective that the Mozart symphony they were playing has no part for a clarinet. It was the clarinetist did it, of course."

Richard smiled. "Winifred and Charlie went their separate ways after seeing Sinjin. They were supposed to meet at Paddington at two. No one, so far as we know, ever saw Winifred again."

"Or heard from her?"

"No. Charlie did hear from her; a note, back at the hotel, where Charlie finally went, saying she couldn't make it. Sorry about that. Looked as though it had been scrawled in a taxi."

"Do you have the note?"

"No. Charlie says she was so upset, she just crumpled it up."

"Did Charlie tell you about the visit when she and Winifred last saw Sinjin?"

"A bit. They chatted, and the old lady said how glad she was to have her will settled, and, of course, the question of Charlotte Stanton's biography. Jolly good cheer all around: yes, George even came in at the end. Had brought a bottle of the bubbly — his phrase — to celebrate. No cloud on the horizon, not even the smallest."

"And I suppose you have made certain it couldn't have been George who did away with Winifred; he's the obvious suspect. Either he's angry about the biography or he's a lunatic who's keeping her prisoner in a basement somewhere."

"It is the comfortable solution, and believe me, I looked into it. My report on that front is very thorough indeed. The problem is, he left Sinjin's the day of the meeting and went off to a golf match in Scotland or Wales, I forget which, and nearly won it, and hundreds of people can testify to his presence almost every hour of the day and night. Also, when I told him Winifred had disappeared, he was obviously astonished. He's either the world's greatest actor or genuine. I tend toward the latter, but good luck to you. I mean it. The report on George is in my office, with all the others. Be my guest."

"I can see you've about had it," Kate said. "And we've finished off all the tea. Thank you for being so patient."

"Not at all," Richard said, rising. "Do call if there's anything else. I really do mean to help you, you know. After talking for a while,

I get a sense of frustration, and I have to move. But that doesn't mean I wouldn't be available, even without those wonderful cookies."

"I understand exactly," Kate said, "and I'm doubly grateful because I do. Thank you, Mr. Fothingale — Richard."

They shook hands collegially at Kate's door.

The next day, a Saturday, Kate set out to visit Ted and Jean Wilkowski. She had thought, for a moment, of asking Leighton to accompany her: "Come Watson, the game's afoot" — or some such drivel. Leighton certainly needed distraction from her fragmented life, torn between no acting, writer's block (that was Kate's guess), and the tedium of word processing, but Kate could not but feel that two would be less likely to win the confidence of Ted and Jean than one. She would have to decide what to do about Leighton.

Kate, as George would have said, "hadn't a clue" what she expected to learn from Jean and Ted, if anything. She could manage to frame none but the most general questions. "Tell me," she wanted to say, "what do you think happened?" But what could they tell her? Driving along, Kate made a mental list, as was her wont — she would commit it to paper at the first opportunity — of some of the homework she must do for this task. First, read the works of Charlotte Stanton, and review what was known of her life. Kate would have to read not only the biography mentioned in Winifred's journal, but whatever else she could find. That was clear enough. In fact, she could pay Leighton to do the research for her: a clever idea, that. "Watson, old girl," she could hear herself saying, "get me a copy of all the articles and books you can find on Charlotte Stanton and her work. If the books are out of print, get them copied from some library. Since Mr. Fothingale, Richard, thinks the answer may be there, we shall look." But why, Kate asked herself, turning off the Taconic and onto Route 23, am I so certain that none of that will make any difference? She brightened up, nonetheless, at the thought of a task for Leighton. "All right," she could hear Leighton saying, "but you've got to promise to keep me informed." Kate had her answer ready: "Watson was your idea; and I beg you to remember that Watson never understood a thing till the very end, when Sherlock Holmes explained it. Be patient, my child."

Glad to have settled her mind on the score of Leighton, Kate felt quite cheerful all the way to Great Barrington, where she decided to park the car and have something to eat before going on to the Wilkowski farm. She found a deli on the main street, advertising health foods and looking as though it belonged on Columbus Avenue in New York. She ordered a mixture of eggplant and avocado on whole wheat pita bread — which Kate did not like, but if one is going to eat health foods, one might as well make a good job of it — and coffee. She took this to a table, and sat munching what seemed to her an extraordinary combination, and trying, without success, to plan what she would say to them at the farm. But plans were not to be hatched. She would have, as one said when preparing to lecture without sufficient preparation, to wing it. It was not an experience Kate often had, or cared for.

And yet, when she met Ted and Jean, she knew that her instinct had been a good one. As they had with Winifred, they sized Kate up and trusted her. Why? Kate wondered, even as she talked with them, happy in that sudden sense of intimacy that only occurs if the chemistry is exactly right. One may often learn to like, even to love, people whom one has not trusted on first sight, but those for whom one feels an instant sense of bonding offer a special brand of friendship or affection.

And this, God knew, was rare enough with a couple. It had been Kate's experience that even when one liked them separately, together couples had their own dynamic that usually short-circuited any impulses of openness.

"Is the A-frame available for viewing?" Kate asked. "No," Jean said. "We've found another farmhand, who's living there. But unless it's general atmosphere you're after, I don't think you'll learn much. Ted and I cleaned out everything of hers; would you like to see that? Let me get it for you, even though I don't know what it can tell you. She had really pared life down to the essentials, Winifred had."

Ted went with Jean to help her, and they returned with two boxes. One, they told Kate, contained clothes and other personal items — toothbrush, toiletries; they had saved everything. "I read detective novels sometimes," Jean smiled, "and who knows what wonderful clue you might find in her toothpaste."

"Mr. Fothingale didn't find anything in her toothpaste, I gather."

"Nothing. Do you want to look through the clothes box?"

"I should probably, on principle, look through both. But let's start with the other box."

"Her journal's gone, of course," Jean said. "There didn't seem to be many other personal papers to speak of. Some financial records, bills, that sort of thing." As she spoke, she was helping Kate to spread papers, books, the occasional magazine, out on the table.

"It doesn't seem right to me," Ted said. "I know we have to try to find out what happened to her. But she was such a private person, and I trusted her. I think she would have trusted me not to go through these things."

"We've had this out, Ted," Jean said. "I don't like it either. But I like her disappearing even less." Jean, after a pause, turned to Kate. "There were a few books from the Lenox library," she said. "I returned them; that seemed only right. But I wrote down the titles."

Kate took the sheet of paper, looked at it a moment — it was clear that Winifred read recent books that interested her, what caught her eye, as well as, one gathered from the Charlotte Brontë novel, some classics. Kate set the list aside, and looked at the other items. They were little enough to be left of a life. Had she a life elsewhere, then? Had she perhaps disappeared into it? Was Cyril, not dead at all, waiting for her in some cottage in darkest Wales? Despite one's scorn of romance, one had to remember, Kate reminded herself, that life was, occasionally, romantic: think of the Ladies of Llangollen. She sorted through writing materials, orderly piles of bills and receipts, and a folder into which, it appeared, Winifred had put what did not come under some other grouping. Kate herself had such a file, labeled *NEC*, for "Not Elsewhere Classified."

These were clippings Winifred had saved, none of them, at a glance, offering much food for speculation, but Kate set them aside for further study. Turning these over, brooding, she came on a piece of folded plastic, perhaps three inches by two inches, with a safety pin on the back. "Now where," Kate asked them, "do you suppose she got that? What is it, and why did she save it?"

"Maybe she thought it would come in handy someday," Ted suggested. "She wasn't a hoarder of things, but she was thrifty."

"Perhaps," Kate said. "It reminds me of something, but I can't think what. Well, I'll take that away too to ponder on." The box revealed little else of interest, even to one wildly on the lookout for clues. "All we can really hope," Kate said, returning to a chair when her search was finished, "is that a study of the works of Charlotte Stanton may reveal something. Fortunately, we have an expert on *her* working with us. It's odd, really, how little Winifred left of her life, which I have the strongest sense was a rich and full one. Most of us gather so much junk in the course of living."

"She was a memorable person," Ted said. (He has thought about the right word for her, Kate sensed, and has come up with that one.) "If we can help in any way, let us know. And if you find her hiding out anywhere, for any reason, tell her she's always got a job with us, and the A-frame to go with it. The kids miss her; even the dogs miss her."

"We all miss her," Jean said, as Kate got ready to leave. "You will let us know if you learn anything about her, won't you? Anything at all?"

Kate, taking her farewell, promised, but not with the hope of having much to report, except, perhaps, some future literary matters about a woman who was not, really, Winifred's aunt. Kate felt intense empathy with the frustrations of Mr. Fothingale.

Eight

The next day, Sunday, Kate devoted to the preparation of her classes, except for an hour spent brooding over the disappearance of Winifred Ashby. At the end of this time, she went to offer her conclusions for Reed's comments. She outlined the whole matter so far, offering him a summary of Winifred's journal, Charlie's letters, and Mr. Fothingale's inconclusive investigations.

"I don't suppose it occurred to anyone to notify the police; they do have a missing person's routine of moderate efficiency."

"Fothingale said they did tell the police," Kate said. "Nothing has come of it. Ted, with Charlie's concurrence, reported Winifred as missing, but the police obviously thought she'd found a better job and just cleared out. She certainly didn't leave behind anything of value, from their point of view."

"I gather she left behind something of value from someone's point of view."

"Now that you ask," Kate said, smiling at him, "she left this, and it's only worth mentioning because I can't figure out what it is. It nudges my memory somehow, but to no practical end." She held out the piece of folded plastic with the pin on the back.

"If you had gone stalking white-collar crime as often as I, my love, you would recognize that: it's a holder for a name tag of the kind used at conventions. They give you a plastic holder like this, and you put your name tag inside it and pin it on your jacket or dress, and wear it as your badge of identification."

"Of course," Kate said. "How odd of me not to recognize it."

"Not odd at all. You are, in my experience, the champion avoider of conventions. When's the last time you attended one, even one given by your professional organization?"

"The MLA. Of course. Reed, you are a genius. Have I told you that lately?"

"Have I given you an idea? What does 'Modern' mean, anyway, in Modern Language Association?"

"Modern Language Association of America

— 'modern' meaning 'not Greek and Latin.' I wouldn't call it an idea; the merest flicker. Have you any other marvelous suggestions?"

"No. Since all the clues seem to point to England — and I hoped to spend your next vacation with you, here — I shall not mention that obvious fact, and I have to admit there doesn't seem to be much else."

As it happened, Kate was having dinner the next evening with a friend from Hunter College, a professor of French whom Kate was inclined to consult when bewildered by the latest communications from France and that country's provocative but dense philosophy. Susan and Kate saw each other from time to time as colleagues do, without any particular end in view, for the fun of it, and to listen to one another's stories of academic outrage. Did men do this? Kate sometimes wondered. Her impression, hardly verified, suggested that her male colleagues either met regularly, to talk, drink, and play squash in the manner of buddies, or not at all, in the manner of male dogs on the same turf.

"Do you happen to know anything about the MLA conventions?" Kate asked her after a while. Her companion opened her blue eyes very wide and stopped chewing.

"A question only you could ask," she finally said. "Don't you even get involved in hiring people?"

"Naturally. But mostly I'm involved with hiring tenured people, and that's usually done in cozy lunches or less cozy dinners on the home front, which is to say the Faculty Club. Is that all one goes for?"

"One goes to give papers, to hear papers, to meet one's distant friends, to have an occasional fling, circumstances permitting, and in my case, to get away from the children in the worst season of the year. None of which, I am to conclude, has ever tempted you."

"I thought one clung to one's children at Christmas, exchanging gifts and humming on about the three wise men."

"Very amusing. Those without children are, I've noticed, honor bound not to reflect on the felicity of their condition; it might discourage the troops. Christmas is hell, and I think they originally scheduled conventions then so that the men, who did the planning, could leave wife with kids, go discuss literature, and carry on in a wonderfully nondomestic and adult way. When the wives started working too, that complicated things.

Josh and I alternate: he goes one year, I go the other. We once tried taking the kids, and our marriage barely held, not that they don't encourage this by letting you bring the kids to the hotel free, an influence, as with so much else, of the new, conservative, pro-family administration in Washington. Some, of course, are clever enough to have husbands or wives in academic disciplines like religion that meet another time of year. What were we talking about?"

"MLA conventions."

"So we were. And you stay home between Christmas and New Year's, having nothing but peace and quiet surrounding you."

"And Reed. That turned out to be his best time of year. Even if someone takes to mass murders, the D.A. manages to put it on hold until the new year dawns. Also, I hate conventions. One seems always to be bumping into the wrong people and missing the others. I did go once, you see, years and years ago. The meetings were all the same: some aged (as it seemed to me then) male professor delivered pompous conclusions while his chosen disciples read papers of unimpeachable boredom. I felt that if someone said something interesting, the whole structure might collapse in a heap. And there was never anywhere to get a drink or a sandwich, or go to the bathroom, unless you went back to your room, which required the use of elevators all going up and never coming down. Did I get the wrong impression?"

"The elevators haven't changed, but everything else has. Those old-type professors complain all the time that their sessions are unattended because placed at the wrong hour or at the same time as one on black autobiography or lesbian poetry in Texas."

"You can't be serious."

"That's just what *they* say. But the newer subjects are exciting as hell, and the old guard is rather put out. They have even — and here you must lower your voice if there are women in the room — they have even been heard to mutter despairingly that there are sessions on the failure of marriages in literature, if you can believe it. Why this sudden interest, anyway? Have they asked you to serve on the program committee?"

"Hardly. But you have inspired me, Susan. Are you telling me that there might have been a session on a minor woman writer such as, for example, Charlotte Stanton?"

"The one who writes all the yummy novels on ancient Greece? Very likely, my dear, though you might try the Popular Culture Association. They don't meet at Christmas, and they have sessions on wonderful things like

136

pornography and poker. I think the police in a southern city actually attended one of their pornography sessions and were plainly seen to fall asleep, having expected filthy pictures and not deconstruction."

"Charlotte Stanton would spin in her grave at the very idea. Though I suppose the Popular Culture types have plastic holders too."

"I gather we are on the bloodhound trail."

"We are. Though it's the merest will-o'-the-wisp. How can I find out what the MLA has had sessions on?"

"Well, you could go to the library and look through the *PMLA* files; the last volume in each year contains the program of that year's convention. Or, being rich and lazy, you could hire someone to do it for you. Or you could go down to the MLA offices and throw yourself on the mercy of the convention folk there. Why not try the latter? It'll give you a sense of the place. But beware: they may think you look promising, and suggest you for a committee."

"Don't people want to serve on their committees?"

"My dear, panting to, for the most part. You get wafted from darkest Kansas or Missouri to New York, put up at a hotel, and locked up in committee rooms at MLA headquarters only for the daylight hours. If you live in New York these temptations are somewhat easier to resist, but never, of course, the temptation to serve the profession."

"And where is French psychoanalytic theory," Kate asked, "with Lacan dead?"

"All the masters, save Derrida, are dead," Susan said. "We are looking to Iragaray and Cixous and Kristeva for great things. Shall we have a bit more wine?"

The headquarters of the Modern Language Association resembles more than anything else the quarters of a large publishing firm or a large legal firm, occupying, as it does, two floors, all with the latest electronic equipment housed in the best of modern taste. Here, as in those similar firms, one steps from the elevator into the presence of a receptionist. It is usual, with lawyers and publishers, for this figure simultaneously to emit feminine come-hitherness and all the welcoming qualities of a guard dog. The MLA, having members rather than clients, becomingly altered this stance with a cheery woman who assumed good intentions, if not always good will — for even members complain — on the part of those who confronted her. For the first time in her encounters with slick offices, Kate did not immediately feel either like a tax auditor or the purveyor of a thousand-page biography of Calvin Coolidge. "Hi," the receptionist said. "What can I do for you?"

"Is it possible to find out about the programs at the conventions in the last few years?"

"Have a seat," the receptionist said. "I like your dress. Someone will help you in a minute."

Kate, sitting down, contemplated the publications displayed. It appeared that, without the bad manners of a publishing firm, this organization went in for publishing. Odd, Kate thought, how in New York one is constantly stumbling on other worlds one knew nothing about, which have been continuing with great energy and influence wholly unaware of one. Is that why I can live nowhere else? Does the good life require the possibility of surprise?

The woman who at this point presented herself to Kate had obviously long since concluded that life, at least in this office, consisted almost wholly of surprises, most of them unpleasant. Her face beautifully combined wariness and concern. "You wanted to ask something about the conventions?" she said, sitting down next to Kate. She had a nice smile.

"Not exactly. I just wondered if you could

help me. I'm eager to know if by any chance there was a session on Charlotte Stanton the novelist at a convention in the last few years. If you want to tell me to go off to the library, I won't blame you. I'm afraid I'm an inveterate taker of shortcuts, which usually means someone else does the work."

"No problem at all," the woman said, rising to her feet with an alacrity that suggested she had expected to be asked, for profound reasons, to move next year's convention to Terre Haute, Indiana. "Come along with me."

She led Kate through a somewhat labyrinthian route to her own office, where there were shelved rows of the journal of the MLA. These were mainly blue. "The brown numbers," Elmira (so she had introduced herself) explained, "come out twice a year: in September, with a directory of members, and in November, with the convention program. You are looking for a meeting in the last few years?"

"I don't even know that," Kate said. "Let's say, starting in 1980 or '81."

"In that case," Elmira said, with a certain expert cheerfulness that made Kate feel guilty — she *should* have gone to the library — "we take down all the convention programs for the eighties, and look under the section titled

'Subject Index to All Meetings.' "

"And just see if there's a listing for Stanton, Charlotte," Kate hopefully concluded.

"Not exactly. Subjects in a broader sense, I'm afraid. If, for example, you wondered if there had been a session on 'Intratextual Repetition: Uses of Doubling and Reiteration,' you would find that under the subheading 'Literary Criticism and Theory,' and then go to the number indicated for details. Which," Elmira said, rapidly flipping pages, "would tell you . . . well, who was giving papers, who was running the session, and where you could send — or could have sent, I should say — for copies of the papers. That was just an example, of course," she added with, Kate sensed, a faint echo of wonder.

Kate encouraged her. "So if I wondered if there was a session on Charlotte Stanton I would look under . . . er . . . 'Twentieth-Century English Literature.' Is that right?"

"That's the idea. Except it's British literature, including the Irish and so forth, but excluding — they have their own category — literature in English other than British or American, and here, under 'Twentieth Century' we find, well, no Charlotte Stanton I'm afraid. But there is 'Jean Rhys: A Commemorative Colloquium,' " she offered, with the air of one trying to make amends. Kate could not but feel that in decency she should have settled for Jean Rhys, not that Elmira, used to dealing with scholars, would have expected any such thing.

"If you'll allow me," Kate said, "I think I've got the idea, and could look through the brown November numbers myself. That is, if I wouldn't be in your way."

"Not at all," Elmira said. "But you understand, there may never have been a session devoted entirely to Charlotte Stanton."

"Alas, yes," Kate said.

"That doesn't mean, of course, that she wouldn't have been the subject of a paper which might have come under some other heading."

"I see what you mean," Kate said. "The subject listed might be 'Modern British or American Authors Writing in English Who Used Greek Settings for Novels of a Popular Persuasion.' That would require rather more careful investigating. I do see that."

"Well," Elmira said, "make yourself at home. I think you'll find this table comfortable; here are the programs for all the conventions since 1980. Would you like a cup of coffee?"

Several cups of coffee and several more convention programs later, Kate had determined that there had *not* been a session on Charlotte Stanton, that, she growled to herself, would have been *too* easy. There had, however, been several sessions in which Charlotte Stanton might have been included, and one in which she was definitely included: that is, her name was listed in the title of one of the papers given under the subject "Oxford Novelists." Since Kate had decided to work backward from the present, she was not even mildly surprised to hit on this session in the earliest (and last) catalogue she examined, 1980. That convention had been held in Houston. She took her discovery, and the few catalogues holding sessions that *might* have included Charlotte Stanton, over to Elmira, who smiled and looked helpful.

"If I might just make copies of these," Kate said, "I shall go away and try not to bother you anymore. Unless," she added, "you'd care to have lunch with me. I am a member in good standing."

Elmira smiled. "I've already determined that," she said. "I also know a little about you. You've been recommended several times to the executive council for positions on some commission or committee, but the impression seems to be that you would turn it down. In

143

fact, I think you have."

"Guilty as charged," Kate said. "But I do support the association as a voice for the humanities in these parlous times. There is that. Let me persuade you to have lunch and you can try to persuade me to do something for the MLA."

"I have to eat lunch anyway," Elmira said, "so it will be a pleasure."

They ended up, after Kate had made her copies and all necessary notes, at a publike restaurant on University Place.

"Do you work all year round on the convention," Kate asked, when they had ordered, "like those people who paint the George Washington Bridge and begin all over again at the other end when they've finished?"

"That's about it," Elmira said. "Except, of course, for attending meetings of the executive council and the directors, and talking to people about past conventions."

"Like me, I know. I'm sorry to be a nuisance, particularly since it may all be in vain; in fact, it very probably is."

"Please don't apologize. In the first place, helping members is my job, and I'm glad to do it. We don't see enough of members, except when they're elected to some committee, or have a complaint. It really is pleasant to talk with someone who isn't indignant because his session was scheduled at eight in the morning, or because she thinks New York hotels' charges for drinks and checking coats are outrageous. As it happens, we agree with the latter, but hardly control the unions and other New York problems. I sometimes think members from out of town blame us for the weather, if bad, and the graffiti in the subway. A request from someone trying to find a paper on a special subject is almost a treat."

"Frankly," Kate said, "I'm less in search of a paper than a person. The person who delivered the paper. And the fact is," she added, "I'm not *really* interested in that person, but in whether he or she happened to meet someone else."

"Perhaps if the other person is a member of the MLA, I might — "

"But I'm pretty sure she isn't. In fact, I know she isn't. That," Kate said with a certain wistfulness, "would be too easy. And, to be honest, wholly unexpected. It's not," she continued, "that I'm not eager to see the paper; I am. In fact, I'm eager to read everything I can about Charlotte Stanton. But I'm looking for someone who might have attended a session on Charlotte Stanton, who might

145

even have registered, though that seems doubt-ful."

"I take it you can't just ask her?"

"No," Kate said regretfully. "That's the problem. She's disappeared altogether."

"Ah," Elmira said. "Well, I don't know how I can help, though if any other plans for sessions concerning Charlotte Stanton are submitted, I'll be glad to let you know. That, of course, wouldn't be for some months yet. We've this year's convention to get through."

"Who chooses the sessions that are ac-cepted?"

"The program committee. You could, you know, take out an advertisement in the *MLA Newsletter;* I think one's due to go to press any day now. You'd have to inquire from the head of publications. Then, if someone knew some-thing, perhaps you could meet at the conven-tion this year; it's in New York."

"Is it indeed?" Kate said. "Is it in New York often?"

"Oh yes. That's our most successful meet-ing place. People always like to visit New York, you see, and we get them special plane rates and hotel rates."

"How many usually come to the conven-tion?"

"In New York, about ten thousand."

"So the extra odd person could certainly escape notice, if he or she wanted to."

"Certainly. On the other hand, one never knows whom one will meet there."

"And nonmembers can register at the convention and get a name tag?" Elmira nodded. "Is there any other way of getting a name tag, or at least one of those plastic holders?"

"Well, we scarcely like to talk about it, but of course the plastic holders are given away, simply piled up in a basket at the registration desk, and someone can certainly put something other than one's own badge into the holder."

"Someone else's badge, for example."

"At the MLA, we prefer not to dwell upon such things."

Kate smiled back. "If I come, I promise to wear my own badge."

"If you preregister, as members can, it will cost less," Elmira said. "Do let me know if there's any more I can do. I seem to remember hearing that you sometimes detect things. Is that what you're doing now?"

"What I'm doing now," Kate said, "is floundering."

Nine

The following morning Kate had a consultation with Leighton. She, Kate, had been brooding on the whole Watson business, and felt disinclined, for her sake and Leighton's, to encourage a caper that could only delay Leighton's commitment to something resembling her eventual life work. At the same time, Kate caught herself up for falling into her brothers' trap: the conviction that one must slot oneself into life before one was too far into one's twenties. If Leighton wanted to drift for a while, perhaps that was right for Leighton. Watson might not be the perfect role for her, but, on the other hand, doing some research on Charlotte Stanton was hardly less fulfilling than word processing in a law firm. Considering the anxieties inherent in aunthood, Kate was glad she had not taken on any more demanding relationship to the young. Motherhood, she suspected, was worse in that one was less capable of cool attitudes. Kate had noticed that parents found it almost impossible to remain unemotional in their advice to their young, and even attitudes of disinterested concern immediately incurred emotional charges from the long-standing parental bank account. Watson and Holmes, not being related, were better able to keep their minds on their jobs.

"I want to know all there is to know about her life," Kate said to Leighton. "It's as simple as that. Of course, I'm looking for clues as to the relation between Winifred and Stanton, but if we just look for one thing we may miss something else even more important."

"Great," Leighton said. "You're prepared to pay me the highest temp fees for reading Stanton stuff. Do I read at home, or in more official surroundings?"

"If the "stuff" is only available in libraries, you'll have to read there. Otherwise, read where you will. I think I'll look at the novels as well — two readings may be more productive than one — but I'll count on you for summaries of all the biographies, criticism, letters, anything published or unpublished you can find. Most of it will have to come from Charlie."

"But you don't want to rely on her summaries."

"No, and only partly to provide you with honorable labor. We may see something different than Charlie sees . . ."

"Or something Charlie doesn't want us to see."

"There is that; the first law of detection is to suspect everyone."

"Except Watson and Holmes, of course."

"Of course. While you are reading and summarizing, I shall be following a wholly different line. We'll compare notes in . . . let's say a week."

"How much do you think I can read in a week?"

"A great deal, you'll find, if you honorably charge only for when you're actually reading. I'm interested also in any accounts of Oxford in the years when Charlotte Stanton was principal; you know, memoirs from students whom she helped over the wall after hours, or fined for going gownless — that sort of thing."

"Perhaps I better make an investigative trip to England," Leighton said.

"First things first," Kate answered dismissively.

Following instructions, Kate sent in her

classified advertisement to the *MLA Newsletter* as indicated on a copy of that publication she had carried away from her morning at the MLA offices. With it she enclosed a check for three dollars a word; she had no problem with the ten-word minimum. Indeed, her powers of concise composition were stretched to the limit. The ad read:

WINIFRED ASHBY: Will anyone who met her in recent years at an MLA convention, either at a session concerned with Charlotte Stanton and her works or elsewhere, please get in touch with Professor Kate Fansler.

In the end, Kate gave her university address and telephone number. She hoped, through the use of the three names, Winifred's, Stanton's, and her own, to flush out those who might, with a more impersonal ad, be inclined not to bother. No doubt she would receive a certain amount of facetious mail, but the risk was, in her view, worth it. She decided, furthermore, to wait to see if the woman who had given the paper on Charlotte Stanton in Houston in 1980 would get in touch with her. If not, Kate could always take the initiative; meanwhile, she had a neat test of the possible range and provacativeness of her ad.

While she waited for the ad to appear, and for the results, if any, she scheduled a long confabulation with Charlie.

This took place in Charlie and Toby's living room, while Toby was at work and where Kate, on her way home from a day's teaching and consulting with students, fortified herself with a martini. Charlie, sipping beer, looked both excited and apprehensive, while Kate felt mainly weary. Perhaps, Kate thought, it's time I had a leave and wrote a book, or undertook some profound investigation full-time. These were characteristically late afternoon thoughts for Kate, always dissolved by the next morning.

"Lives of leisure always look so attractive from the outside," Kate said, "but less so from inside, I've often noticed. Do you like your unstructured life: no office, no routine unless self-imposed, no people about? I gather, since you left Dar and Dar so precipitously, you longed for leisure. Has it been all you expected?"

"I left precipitously because I didn't want to work there any longer once Toby and I were definitely committed to one another; he was having trouble telling anyone about us, which I thought, rightly as it turned out, was at least partly because I was in the office. So I simply decamped, and except for Leighton, they forgot all about me. I did realize that if we met later at some office party, people from the firm might recognize me (although office workers are often unrecognizable out of context), but I just wanted to let time pass. So far, it has passed very nicely. And I did still have Toby there to deal with the Sinjin end — the two wills, you know."

"You didn't come to Larry's party for the associates."

"No, I'm biding my time, but that seemed a good one to miss in any case. Of course, I didn't know you'd be there. To answer your question, I've been so busy worrying about Charlotte Stanton, I haven't had time to miss having a daily structure in my life. But unless you're successful as a writer — that is, have some feedback coming in from books you've written and expect to write and are writing — I think it could be a mighty lonely life and even a depressing one. One of the advantages of writing a biography, of course, is that one has to beetle off and talk to folks about one's subject."

"And Winifred Ashby was one of the folks you beetled off to talk to."

"Yes. Except, as you'll recall, Sinjin wanted

to find her too. Hence George, and the whole bit you've read."

"Why do you think Toby was uncomfortable about your relationship? And that, let me hasten to add, is not a question I have any business asking, so just tell me to stick to Winifred and mind my own business if you like."

"He's quiet, and doesn't like talking about himself, partly a male hang-up, and partly lack of practice. Also, I'm younger than he is, and Toby's always scorned men who ran off at sixty with younger women. Then, having grown up with the likes of the Fanslers, he's class-conscious (though he'd deny it with his dying breath), and senior partners don't take up with office workers, or at least don't live with them. There's probably more, but will that do for starters?"

"That'll do nicely, thank you. My policy is: if you wonder, ask; but don't be offended if you don't get an answer. And pick yourself up if you get knocked to the ground."

"A good policy, obviously. Meanwhile, back on the farm, has anyone a clue?"

"What you might call one meager clue, which I'd rather not talk about now, if that's okay by you. What happens to the money if Winifred turns out to be dead?"

"Sinjin's money? It goes to George."

"According to your letters, Winifred agreed to split the money with George."

"Right. When Sinjin wanted to see Winifred and Toby couldn't find her is when all this began."

"And you went and applied for a job at the firm; in fact, you went to the firm to see Toby in the first place because of your interest in Charlotte Stanton."

"Right again. I'd planned for a very long time to write a biography of her. It wasn't that hard to find out where her will was made, or to get in touch with Sinjin. After that, tracking Toby down was a natural. Are you suspecting a deep plot?"

"Not in the least; just testing my aging brain. Have you been able to find much written about Stanton, by academics or anyone else?"

"Not a great deal of value, apart from the biographies. With all this new data processing, on-line retrieval, and whatnot, you can get a pretty thorough picture of what's been done, except for the occasional piece hidden away in some obscure journal. You can also find how often her name's been mentioned in the major newspapers, and where and when. It's no wonder most of the academics are into theory these days: research isn't the attractive rummage act it used to be. Interpretation is more challenging, and quite beyond the range of computers, so far."

"How do you interpret her life, if you can trust me enough to tell me? I promise not to sneak off and write a book on anything even remotely connected to Charlotte Stanton."

"Part of it's clear enough: she was a rigorous scholar, a linguist, a philologist even. She maintained the highest standards of everything from social behavior to scholarly endeavors when she was principal, and her mien was certainly severe, to say the least. Yet she wrote these passionate tales of Athens, which the public ate up in great gobbles, all about men loving one another and leading manly honorable lives. There's a theory that her novels supported her passion for philology, but I don't buy that for a minute. One writes novels because one wants to, whatever other reasons there may be."

"And her love life?"

"*The* question. She was unusual for that time, though not perhaps in that place, in having close women friends. Naturally, there were endless rumors that she was lesbian, but that's just because she dressed badly, wore her hair unbecomingly, and got fat. There's a feeling abroad and ever was, I find, that women who have no interest in attracting men are supposed to be lesbian; as though most of my gay women friends weren't spiffy dressers. Women like Stanton are, half the time, just uninterested in clothes, and, in the course of their professional lives, if they're intellectuals and academics, they meet and talk with men all the time. Most of the Oxford dons I've met, for what it's worth, are likelier to have a good conversation with the likes of Stanton than with their wives."

"Winifred's journal, about Cyril's mother, certainly suggests that."

"Exactly. The problem with Stanton, really, is that one can establish plenty of negatives; it's the positives that keep evading one, such as why did she spend those years rattling around instead of going right to work for her B. Litt? Did she have affairs, and if so, with whom? And, last but best, what relation was Winifred to her, that she should invite her to Oxford for the summers?"

"There's not a single clue to that?"

"Not so far. One of the ironies is that I thought we might hypnotize Winifred and perhaps pick up a clue or two, but now that's past praying for, or so it seems. I mean, something might have emerged behind what I think is called a screen memory; it was worth a try. The most galling thing for me, of course, is all the questions I *didn't* ask Winifred when I had the chance. How was I to know she'd disappear like that? I *could* have asked her if she'd heard from Stanton in those years, but I was looking forward to long conferences and many questions. Do you think someone could have kidnapped her who wanted to write a biography of their own? They'll brainwash her, make her forget her past, and then let her go. Speaking of hypnosis."

"Too bad Cyril's mother isn't living."

"Both his parents are dead now; the father died before Cyril, and the mother just a few years ago. Talk of dead ends!"

"Could you lend me all of Stanton's novels, just for a short time?" Kate asked. "I promise to return them promptly, their condition unchanged."

"Of course. I have all first editions, so it is an act of trust."

"Which I much appreciate. For some reason, I'm eager to read them as they were originally published; a not quite atrophied scholarly instinct, no doubt."

Kate carried off seven novels, determined to read them through from beginning to end. It might lead nowhere; it would probably lead nowhere. But if one was a professional student of literature, and a teacher of same, one ought to have some faith in the revelatory powers of a text. Or so, hailing a taxi and clutching her bag of books to her, Kate self-righteously told herself. One needed a profound reason for reading novels at the expense of one's proper work.

Reading the novels when not, perforce, otherwise engaged, took Kate a week, at the end of which Leighton also had completed her appointed task. That is, she had photocopies of an amazing number of articles, or so it seemed to Kate, most of them newspaper and magazine accounts of a popular and gossipy nature complete with Stanton portrait; a few ponderous, speculative, and analytic; none of them, in Leighton's opinion, worth a cup of warm spit. Kate, glancing through them, was inclined to agree with her.

"Was there anything at all in what you found," Kate asked Leighton, "to indicate the basis of her relationship with Winifred? To even suggest that such a relationship existed?"

"Meaning," Leighton said, settling down in Kate's living room, "have we any reason, apart from Winifred's journal, to believe any of that stuff about her childhood in Oxford, her relation to Stanton, the whole bit?"

"You're being far too smart for Watson," Kate said. "I'm supposed to raise that question at the very end, having treasured it as the operative clue all along."

"But have we any reason?" Leighton persisted.

"A great many, unfortunately. Mr. Fothingale checked it all out in England, asked around, spent a good deal of time and money — Charlie's money, I might point out. There are a number of records of Winifred's presence in Cyril's family house, the aunt did have an apartment there, and the aunt did mention Winifred in her will. Sinjin became her literary executor and it was understood that she would pass on part of the royalties to Winifred in her turn. Sinjin was at Oxford with Stanton, and they remained friends, so she must have known all about Winifred. Fothingale met her, not to mention George. And then there are the people on the farm."

"I don't doubt that Winifred existed. But suppose her journal was written by someone else and planted."

"I think you are being somewhat romantic about this investigation, overdoing the Baker Street influence. I doubt if Charlie or anyone else could have forged that journal. Charlie has that dogged manner of the born re-searcher — the sort who write biographies by collecting all the facts, I mean, not by rear-ranging them in a new and provocative way."

"Odd she should have taken up with Toby."

"Leighton, you're going to suggest she killed Toby's wife next."

"Can you be sure she didn't, just for argu-ment's sake?"

"Just for argument's sake, I can." "So you have had your suspicions?" "Not really. I be-lieve in checking everything out, insofar as that is possible. In my experience, it isn't pos-sible very far. People don't go through life leaving records of everything, or writing someone about it in great detail, complete with unconscious motives. Where was I?"

"Getting irritable because I'm suspecting Charlie."

"Oh, Leighton, do behave. If you'll remove yourself from the ambience of Baker Street, and return to our living room with your sense of reality intact, you'll realize that Charlie would have had to engineer a conspiracy of in-credible proportions, not to mention vamping Toby, which might not be too hard in one sense, but would not be easy in another. Toby is no fool."

"Which may be why he wanted you looking into this. The smallest gnawing of doubt, which you would either explain or dispel."

"There is the question of why both these women should have made wills in the U. S., instead of in London. But they left total records of them in London, and since Winifred was an American it makes a certain amount of sense. And after Winifred, the money goes to George. You're not going to suggest that Charlie is in cahoots with George, or is this your day for weaving fantasies so why not let them rip?"

"What did you find in the novels?" Leighton asked, ignoring this.

"Not much. A clue here and there, one sensed, but like so many clues, probably belonging to another treasure hunt. She writes of Greece, bringing many of the mythical and historical characters to life, inventing stories for them, characters like Theseus, Plato, Ariadne, Alexander, Euripides. All the protagonists are men; the only women characters of substance are seen negatively, like Ariadne, for example, who is made to become the worst sort of monster of male imagination, gnawing on pieces of human flesh. Yet the men are on the whole idealized, harsh fighters but loving, with intense loyalties to one another."

162

"Your impression is that she was interested only in men?"

"It may be that," Kate said. "But I get a sense rather that she has despaired of women, that despite all that she and some of her contemporaries proved about women's capacities, women still insist on centering their lives on trivialities, domestic virtues, and the admiration of men. So in her fictions she gives all the virtues to men, and relishes exiling women to the margins of meaningful life. This is probably all fancy," Kate added impatiently.

"It certainly doesn't tell us much about Winifred."

"No. Except that they shared a tendency to idealize male life. But then, so did Charlotte Brontë. In *Shirley* Caroline Helstone says, 'I should like an occupation; and if I were a boy, it would not be so difficult to find one.' Why struggle with female characters and love plots, when you can write of everything else if you will only write of men?"

"I see your point, but that hardly proves they were related."

"Hardly. There's a scene in one of the books where a young man's father has gone off to war somewhere, leaving his pregnant young wife in his son's care with clear instructions: if the baby is a girl, kill it, expose it. If it's a boy, keep it. The baby is a girl, but the young man takes pity on the young wife and lets her keep it. Shades of Winifred?"

"Surely one didn't commit infanticide in twentieth-century England."

"I was speaking metaphorically, nonsensically — oh what does it matter?" Kate said, getting up to pace the room. "I think," she concluded, "we'd better let the whole thing rest for a while. At least for a few weeks. All we have, really, is an absence. No Winifred. We have no motive, no evidence that she's more than disappeared, no person whom one could suspect without the wildest of fantasies. Charlie, Ted and Jean, George, Toby — I ask you, who cares enough to kill or kidnap her? Back to word processing, I fear, Leighton."

"Well," Leighton said, rising from her horizontal position on the couch, "I've made enough off you to keep me for a week or two. Maybe something will turn up, meanwhile. Keep in touch."

And Kate returned the novels to Charlie, filed the articles away, and gave her attention to the gathering demands of the academic semester's last weeks.

Ten

The response to Kate's ad in the *MLA News-letter* was, numerically speaking, altogether satisfactory. The number of scholars interested in English writers who had been at Oxford in the twentieth century astonished Kate and pleased her. That almost everyone who knew anything of Oxford in those years knew something of Charlotte Stanton indicated to Kate that the condition of so-called minor writers was not always as obscure as she, and no doubt others, had supposed. As principal of a college, and a scholar renowned in her field, Stanton was a personage. That she also wrote popular fiction was simply ignored; so Kate gathered from perusing her letters and the articles enclosed with them that referred, often only in a footnote, to Stanton. The writing of novels, like any other barely acceptable anomaly in one's private life, was one's own affair. And, as Kate already knew, even an interest in a "modern" writer like Joyce or Lawrence or Woolf, had, in those years, been countenanced at Oxford only if confined to one's publications, and not considered the subject of lectures or tutorials. All that had, to be sure, changed in the seventies. But by then one was well into the postmodern period, and the moderns, having become history, were acceptable as an academic pursuit. Odd, really, about periodization. But at least it had allowed Stanton to write her novels without encroaching upon the very literature Oxford deemed worthy of study.

Kate read the letters with delight. Despite the fact that Winifred Ashby's name had appeared in large type at the beginning of the ad, most of those who wrote to Kate referred only to Charlotte Stanton. Kate had the sense that they were eager to talk to, be in correspondence with, anyone who knew Stanton and her works. The loneliness of the scholar, particularly one devoted to a minor figure, is little recognized. Some who wrote were wags, either pleased on general principles with the chance to be facetious or, having met or heard of Kate, happy for the chance to josh her in what they hoped was a witty and pointed man-

166

ner. Quite often, Kate had to admit, it was. Kate had long noticed that requests for information and letters to the editor were read with rather more attention than the regular articles that constituted the main part of the publication — any publication. Aside from the letters inspired by ads in general and Kate's in particular, and those concerned only with Charlotte Stanton, there remained a few of special interest.

The first of these, to Kate's satisfaction, was from the woman who had presented the paper on Stanton in Houston in 1980. She said that she was not certain if she had met the right Winifred Ashby, but that she thought it likely. If Kate was in no particular hurry, she added, the woman would be happy to meet with Kate and talk with her at the forthcoming MLA convention in New York. Kate, who believed a good deal more could be learned through freewheeling conversation than from a letter, and who didn't think it fair, in any case, to impose the writing of so time-consuming a letter on a stranger, responded by inviting the woman, named Alina Rosenberg, to her, Kate's, room for a drink. Kate had already determined to reserve a room at a hotel for the purpose of meeting people, even if she did not sleep there.

Her determination to attend the MLA convention had been reinforced by the other letters. One, anonymous, again offered to meet Kate at the MLA, and said, mysteriously and provocatively, that Kate might, or might not, learn something of interest to her. *What* was not specified. A third letter, to Kate's astonishment and delight, said the writer had known Winifred Ashby as an adolescent in Ohio, and would that be of any interest to Kate? He also would be attending the convention, and would be glad to talk with Kate there.

Which left Kate with little to do apart from finishing up the term, with all the last-minute rush that entailed, planning her interviews at the MLA, and breaking the news to Reed that she intended not only to attend the convention but to reserve a hotel room. She was quite prepared to invite him to share it with her or, in the face of any strong objections on his part, to refer in her most ladylike manner to recent Fansler law parties for associates. Had he not dragged her to that, her need to attend the MLA convention would never have arisen.

Reed, however, turned out to be amused. He doubted whether a night spent in the hotel room would hold any special delights; might he not await her at home? "I hope," he added, "you have already received your name card and plastic holder." Kate told him that the plastic holder would be acquired at the convention, and that she looked forward eagerly to possessing it. Reed grinned.

Kate did not register at her hotel, which had turned out to be the Sheraton — foreign languages were at the Hilton — until the evening of the first day of the convention, having been warned by those of long experience that the lines for registering would be endless in the afternoon. As it was, she had a wait and was enthralled by the activity in the lobby — the calls of recognition, the glances at name cards, some furtive, some direct and challenging; the sadness of those lost, or alone, or anticipating an interview on which might depend all the events of the next few years, if not their lives. The men were assured, their faces unexpressive, their manner verging on the pompous. The women looked either weary or delighted to meet some acquaintance, more exposed, Kate decided, willing to risk more in a personal way, as though greeting the wrong person would not be a matter of moment. Never an advocate of the theory of separate cultures for the genders,

Kate nonetheless often felt that a visitor from Mars might immediately conclude that men and women were different species.

Her room, when she achieved it, having with some difficulty manipulated the electronic card with which hotels have replaced the key, proved to be as anonymous and efficient as she had hoped. There were several chairs and a table; the bed, if not slept in, would (as a receptacle for coats) offer little embarrassment to Kate. One scarcely liked to entertain total strangers in what appeared to be the ambience of one's private life. Still, rooms at conferences must be accepted for all purposes, including the establishment of new relationships, sexual or not. She left a small suitcase she had brought as evidence of the room's being occupied — Susan had told her that having once, like Kate, taken a room for daytime use, she had returned after an evening session to use the bathroom, and found the room turned over to a couple in no condition to be aroused, as they were, by her imperious knocking — and went out to buy some liquor, club soda, and pretzels. On her way, she stopped to pick up her plastic holder, and to slip her name tag into it. The tag at its top declared: MODERN LANGUAGE ASSOCIATION, NEW YORK, NY, and the dates of the

170

conference. KATE FANSLER and the name of her university had been printed below in bulletin-type letters three-quarters of an inch high. Usually opposed to tags and flaunted identification — had this been one of the reasons she had avoided conventions? — she now wore it prominently. If one advertised for information, one should make the target of that information readily recognizable.

Waiting her turn at the liquor store, Kate looked through her program to see what, if anything, she might attend that evening. At nine o'clock, one page alone of the program offered her a choice between "Phenomenological Literary Theory After Deconstruction," "The Image of Night in Sixteenth-Century Spanish Mysticism," and "Theory of Women's Autobiography." Might the last give her a clue about Winifred Ashby? After noting the name of the meeting rooms, Kate reached her turn to buy her liquor and other supplies; she carried them to her room and found the red light on her phone blinking. Calling the operator, Kate discovered that she had several messages, but that they were written and must be picked up at the desk in the lobby. After confronting the elevators, overcrowded and infrequent, Kate, once in one, listened entranced to the conversations and watched the eager reading of name tags. Her own, it appeared, occasioned an exclamation from a woman standing nearby. *Her* tag, Kate saw, read "Alina Rosenberg." Kate greeted her eagerly as they were ejected, with the emerging crowd, from the elevator. Achieving a corner of the crowded lobby, they shook hands.

"I was just on my way to leave you a message," Alina said, "to arrange a meeting. Are you busy now?"

"Not at all," Kate said, always eager to seize the moment, but with an instant's regret for possible illumination on the question of phenomenological literary theory after deconstruction. "Would you like to come to my room?"

"That would probably be best," Alina said. "I've got a roommate." Once again, they approached the elevators, hopefully pushing buttons. Attention to their conversation meant that they had not forced their way to the front of approaching elevators, and so failed to squeeze onto several. "Surely," Kate said, when they had finally flattened themselves into one, "this is the worst part of the convention."

"You must be in a very fortunate situation if you can think that," a voice answered her, and Kate felt ashamed. "It's a slave market, the

172

MLA convention," Susan had told her, and Kate blushed now at the easy assumption of her own security. So many of those in the humanities were, Kate knew, jobless, though full of talent and willing to go anywhere.

"Funny about that," Alina said, when they were seated in Kate's room. "I thought the woman who may have been Winifred Ashby was looking for a job, too, and I asked her if she had any interviews scheduled. She seemed puzzled by the question, which puzzled me in turn. Then, I'm afraid, I rather lost track of her."

"I'd like to hear all about the session in Houston, if you don't mind telling me," Kate said.

"Not a bit. The Houston convention was rather ghastly and, therefore, memorable in more ways then one. We went to Houston because Illinois and Louisiana hadn't ratified the ERA, and while I agreed wholly with that decision, I was more than a little startled to find myself in Houston, or even to realize that Texas had ratified it. I later learned they would have liked to retract their ratification, which shows how odd life is. One would certainly have preferred New Orleans or Chicago."

"And you think Winifred Ashby came to

hear your paper on Charlotte Stanton?"

"Yes. She came up afterwards to say she'd enjoyed the paper. Odd the things you remember. I suppose it was because she'd caught my eye earlier, sitting there listening so intently. Tall, dressed rather elegantly in pants and a shirt, early forties, give or take a few years. Does that sound like your Ashby woman?"

"It does. As we know, she had a great interest in Charlotte Stanton, who was her honorary aunt, and with whom she spent summers at Oxford."

"But you've lost track of her."

"Altogether, I'm afraid. That's why anything you can tell me will be so helpful. Might I, by the way, see your paper on Charlotte Stanton?"

"Of course; I've brought you a copy."

"Do you remember much about the other papers?"

"Not a good deal. Frankly, I didn't find them either interesting or relevant. All the other Oxford novelists were men; but you must have seen the program. I'm afraid there was a certain scorn for my female popular novelist, though I think most of the audience was there to hear about her — and perhaps about Robert Graves."

"They both wrote popular novels about ancient Greece and Rome, didn't they?"

"Well, there is that, though I don't remember the point being made at the time. It was one of those panels where the panelists don't really interact; we each did our own thing, and answered questions addressed to us individually at the end. There was a lot of coming and going among those who attended the session — that always happens at the MLA, but this seemed even more so. That's why I first noticed Ashby; she just sat there, toward the front, listening, giving one that sense of being attended to which is so rare and so pleasant."

"And I'm very grateful to you," Kate said. "Can I offer you something to drink? I've stocked up."

"Thank you, wine would be nice," Alina said. "The fact is," she added, as Kate handed her a glass, "I always find these conventions very depressing; each year I swear I won't come again. But then, in the part of Idaho I come from, there aren't any decent bookstores; I like to see the book exhibits, and to hear what's going on in some of the areas I'm interested in. And, since I'm working on a woman author, it is good to meet others interested in women's writing. There's little of that at home either. But somehow, it's all so competitive and discouraging. I wonder often what Charlotte Stanton would have made of it."

"Have you worked mainly on her life or her writings?"

"Both, really. I'm concentrating on her work, with just a chapter on her life, but one can't help going back and forth, particularly now when that sort of thing is becoming more acceptable; not like the New Criticism days when people weren't supposed to have lives, or to have put them in their work."

"Did you know that someone named Charlotte Lucas is writing a biography of Stanton?"

"Oh, God, don't tell me. No, I didn't. But that's how it goes. Two people writing books on the same subject is always happening."

"I didn't mean to worry you. I'm sure in these cases each of the books has something different to say. I only mentioned it not to seem to be holding anything back."

"Well," Alina said, "she's probably able to go to England every year, and do proper research. That's not possible for me. But then, the publisher I'm writing for isn't that demanding. It's a sort of introductory book, though I hope to make it good."

"You will," Kate said, thinking: What fortunate lives we lead, Charlie and I. Thinking:

Perhaps Charlie will get in touch with her, and share some of the goodies. But Kate only said: "Did you ever see the woman who might have been Winifred Ashby again at the convention in Houston?"

"I met her once in the lobby as one does," Alina said. "We smiled, and she told me again how much she had liked my paper. That's when I asked her if she was there for interviews. But I didn't get the impression she wanted to hang around and talk. She seemed on her way somewhere. I'm sorry there isn't more. I'm afraid none of this has been the least helpful."

"You're wrong," Kate said. "It's been immensely helpful, and I'm grateful to you. From what you know of Stanton's life and novels, do you think she ever had a child?"

Alina stared. "Good heavens, no. Her whole life seemed a careful avoidance of marriage and children, as far as I can tell. Whether she didn't have the opportunity to marry the right person, as we used to think, or chose not to marry, which I now believe, she clearly had decided to hell with ironing men's shirts and darning their socks. Probably," Alina added, with more sophistication than Kate had yet seen in her, "I'm what the psychoanalysts call projecting. Saying to hell with it wasn't possible in my day."

"I don't suppose it was ever easy; it may not even have been a conscious choice. Have you ever wondered about Jane Austen?"

Alina let this pass as a rhetorical question. She rose slowly, putting down her glass and gathering up her belongings. "Thanks for the drink," she said, "and for the conversation. Get in touch with me if I can be of any further help. I've written out my room number and my home address. It's a pleasure to talk to you, and I'd welcome another opportunity." Which Kate, seeing her to the door, and accepting the piece of paper with Alina's address and room number, took to mean: There aren't many like you in my part of Idaho. We New Yorkers, Kate would have liked to tell her, but didn't, are a breed apart, often scorned, sometimes cherished. She wished there was something especially nice she could do for Alina, but she was afraid the generosity would have to be Charlie's. Because she had met Alina in that fortuitous way, Kate had not picked up her messages. She set out once again in search of them, bracing herself anew for the elevators. "Just remember," Susan had told her, "don't complain too loudly about the elevators. If they hear you, they stop between floors and can't be moved for hours, or simply sulk and refuse to open their doors."

Kate had a number of messages by the time she retrieved them, most of them jocular comments on her presence by friends and colleagues who had seen her name posted on the "Who's Where" notice board. But two of them had to do with her Ashby quest: one, from the anonymous correspondent, said: "I'll knock on your door ten o'clock on the first night of the convention, the 27th. If you can't see me then, don't aswer — obviously, the result also if you aren't there." Kate looked at her watch. She had five minutes to brave the elevators and return to her room. The other message, from the man who had known Winifred in Ohio, simply left his room number, saying he would be interviewing all day, but would be glad to see Kate for breakfast in his suite on December 29th or 30th, if she would only leave a message to let him know. Kate observed that the important assignations of the convention took place at very odd hours indeed. Kate never met anyone for breakfast, for any reason, a policy like so many, as she had discovered in her later years, she would have to abandon. It occurred to Kate that she was down to practically no policies at all, perhaps a blessing.

She had gained her room two minutes before the knock came, and she opened her door to a tall and conventionally handsome man who shook her hand, said he hoped she had something for him to drink, and announced that he had heard of her. Whether this was a compliment to him or her was unclear as, Kate feared, would be the motives of most of what he said. His whole attitude and body language declared what was his major pursuit at this convention and all others. As he spoke, Kate realized that his avidity for observing the sexual encounters of others equaled his delight in his own. He wore a wedding ring, thus confirming Kate's more cynical views on marriage. But, she reminded herself, this was all instantaneous supposition. He might prove Jane Austen's dictum about the unreliability of first impressions. As he accepted his drink, however, and began to speak at length, it became clear that first impressions, in some cases, still held.

"May I safely assume," he asked Kate, "that you're not looking for evidence in a divorce case?" Kate stared at him. "I thought not," he said, "but one must be sure. Bitch that the woman is, I wouldn't want to aid her in taking her husband for a bundle."

"Can there be some misunderstanding?"

Kate asked. "I have the sense we're not talking about the same people."

"Ashby, you said in your cute little ad. Winifred Ashby. Do you suppose there are more than one of them, both connected to the tacky Miss Charlotte Stanton?"

Kate still couldn't believe it. "What age is your Winifred Ashby?" she asked. Surely this man must be speaking of a young woman.

"Pushing fifty, if you ask me. Well, forty-four or forty-five. I'll say this for the guy, he doesn't go for them young and cute. Unlike some of us," he added with a complicitous grin. Kate, who was glad to hear it, said nothing.

"Don't misunderstand me," he said, holding out his glass for a refill. "While my motives are definitely sinister, I can probably help you to find your Ashby woman. But I do need a little encouragement. Besides alcohol," he added, as Kate took his glass. Not for the first time in a long academic career, Kate found herself in the position of wanting information from a person to whom she would dearly have loved to convey her true opinion. Uncertain whether she was about to be blackmailed or merely appealed to as a womanly woman, Kate remained silent, an attitude in women, she had noticed, that men tended to interpret in their own favor.

"Okay," he said. "I see you're in a tough spot. The fact is, so am I. Maybe we can help each other." Kate's silence now was true, unfeigned amazement. "The fact is, I badly want library privileges at your university, and I think you could get them for me if you put your mind to it. Either you could shoehorn me into one of the famous university seminars or you could sponsor me as a visiting postdoctoral scholar; I'll leave the method up to you. And even," he added with, Kate had to admit, a certain perspicacity, "though you probably consider me the lowest form of life, I promise not to steal any library books. My intentions toward libraries are strictly honorable."

This, Kate thought, is not happening to me. These things don't happen in real life, we all know that. "I don't even know your name," she said, since some response was required. And, she would have liked to add, since you are given to sending anonymous letters, to say nothing of this conversation, I'm not sure I want to.

"I see your problem. Actually, I came to sum you up. Clearly, you're an honorable type. If you promise something, you perform it, however awkward it may be. I have an aunt by marriage like that. Her cat had kittens, and she insisted upon keeping the ugliest one. She said, when asked why, that she had promised it when it was born to keep it. That's your type, I'd say at a guess."

Kate found herself remembering her early views of academe, the reasons she had wanted so fervently to be a part of it. Because all the men (her teachers then had been all men) seemed so honorable, so finely tuned to the niceties of courtesy. And nothing that has happened seems to change that expectation, she thought. I'm like a woman who goes on believing in romance, having been deserted by fifteen men at regular intervals. "I might have another," the man said. "Can I fix you one?"

"Thanks," Kate said, "I don't drink." With the likes of you, she silently added.

"Okay. Well here's my bit of news, for what it's worth, and you know what I hope it's worth. You might look up a dame called Mary Louise Heffenreffer, Biddy to her friends — of whom she has damn few. She's maybe forty-five and, though I hate to say it, gorgeous. One of those bodies." He glanced at Kate. "Not unlike yours, I have to admit, except fuller in certain places. And she's a dresser. Do you know those stores here called

Charivari? She looks like any moment of any day, she might be in their window. And their clothes are not cheap, let me tell you. In short, she has style. And sex." And, Kate thought, she wanted no part of you, which suggests that she has taste as well.

"Yes," he said, "exactly what you're thinking. Maybe women scorned are dangerous, but that's because Shakespeare didn't get around to describing men who've been . . ." He decided not to use the phrase that came readily to mind, though Kate could have supplied it. Despicable men were frequently mealymouthed when not with their buddies. "She could have her choice, I grant you that. But she couldn't keep her husband in tow. They're both professors, by the way, in some artsy-fartsy college near here. And you know who she lost her husband to — not legally, of course, but in body and spirit, which is what matters? Your, or somebody's, Winifred Ashby. Now, how's that for an unexpected answer to an ad in the *MLA Newsletter?* My name, by the way, is Stan Wyman, in case you need to check me out, to establish that I'm not an unaffiliated madman." And knowing, Kate had to grant him, the line on which to leave, he walked through the door, snapping it to behind him.

Kate sat in her chair, stunned. Winifred Ashby as the object of a jealous wife, and a gorgeous one at that? Could Stan Wyman be quite simply a lunatic? Well, as they used to say, "It pays to advertise," a phrase, as Kate was fond of pointing out, invented by Dorothy L. Sayers, but widely credited, like many of Sayers's observations about Dante's *Inferno*, to American entrepreneurs. Removing the bedspread, in the light of Susan's strictures, and leaving her case prominently displayed, Kate put the liquor in the closet (another Susan suggestion), and departed the room with loving thoughts of Reed, with whom she decidedly would like to have a drink. On her way out of the hotel, she paused to leave a message for the Ohio letter writer that she would meet him for breakfast in his suite on December 29th. Tomorrow morning, at least, she would not have to rise at dawn, but once having risen, would be free to attend a session on something or other — perhaps, in deference to the unfailingly helpful Susan, on the further ranges of semiotics.

Eleven

Kate arrived home to find Reed and Leighton deep in conversation. With infinite tact, they greeted her as a returned warrior, and plied her with spiritual and material reinforcement: conversation and drink. Kate always found it cleared her brain to tell Reed what had happened, and Leighton, after all, was entitled to know. Suppose Holmes had had a wife? Watson, of course, did have one, but since he deserted her for the hearth and company of Holmes, the question of her part in the detection never arose. The hell with it, Kate thought; I hate analogies. She told them all that had happened, especially about the detestable Stan Wyman, who had, of a sudden, cast Winifred Ashby in a wholly unexpected and uncharacteristic light.

"That awful man is probably making the

186

whole thing up," Leighton said, with all the knowledge of a generation widely experienced in these matters. "He sees it as a way to make you feel beholden so he can get his damn library card, and crawl his way into your acquaintanceship. It will probably turn out he wouldn't know Winifred Ashby from Chris Evert Lloyd. No doubt," she added, as Kate opened her mouth, "he's got it in for the Heffenreffer dame. But if I were you, I'd be damn careful about falling into his kitten-anecdote trap: honorable type indeed. The man is infuriating."

"He certainly sounds it," Reed agreed. "Perhaps this is one of the less beneficent effects of personal ads. For years, it's been a well-known ploy. You remember that Holmes used to follow the personals column with great interest."

"Is everyone around here becoming a Holmes nut?" Kate rather ungraciously asked. "Because, frankly, I'm getting rather tired of the old boy. It's all very well for you two to sit here discussing the world and chortling away, but you've no idea what it's like at one of those conventions. Unless one is madly gregarious, with appointments for every moment, or interviewing all through the day — most of the department chairpersons are chained to the radiator, poor dears — or on the sexual prowl, conventions force one to alternate wildly between crowds and the most depressing kind of solitude, as though one were in a foreign country with no proper money, and no place to sit except in one's hotel room. I'm going to bed, and I don't wish to be awakened for anything less startling than the reappearance of Holmes himself. If you two think of something profound, leave me a note, which I'll read upon awakening."

Leighton blew her aunt a kiss.

On the next day Kate, as she had predicted, awoke very late indeed. There was a cheerful note from Reed, to wish her well and tell her that he and Leighton had agreed upon the suggestion that she simply skip the rest of the convention; it wasn't, they felt, doing anything positive for her disposition or for the investigation. She had succeeded only in encountering one of the more unfortunate types who haunt such events, and had accomplished little else. Reed, concluding on an affirmative note, looked forward to seeing her for dinner.

But Kate, despite this excellent advice, went off to the convention, though not to attend a session on semiotics or anything else of her choice; she had decided to stalk Mary Louise Heffenreffer, known to her friends as Biddy. Consulting the list of "Program Participants," Kate discovered that Heffenreffer, Mary L., was delivering a paper on Pulci in a session on historical aspects of the Italian Renaissance epic. Kate, who was beginning to feel that the major revelation of this convention was her ignorance of everything, could only learn that Pulci had written an epic called *Il Morgante,* of which Byron had translated the first canto. She was driven to telephoning a colleague, fortunately a man of humor and generosity, who told her a bit more about Pulci, adding that no one but Italian scholars knew anything about him, and that no doubt the Heffenreffer paper would be exceedingly interesting in taking up the historical aspects of Pulci's work and its influence on Ariosto and sixteenth-century comic epics. Thus armed, Kate went off to the session expecting the whole proceedings to be conducted in Italian. But Ms. Heffenreffer spoke not only in elegant English, but clearly and, it appeared from the discussion, somewhat controversially. Kate, who, like so many modernists, found it difficult to understand how anyone could get herself excited over the motives of a writer dead five hundred years and writing about a society wholly mysterious, pondered Heffenreffer rather than Pulci. Kate's visitor of last night had been right: she was gorgeous, though Kate had long since become accustomed to the fact that women scholars were no longer dowdy by definition, nor unsexy by decision. Still, by the age of forty-five most scholars of either sex, like most people in any profession, began to sag a bit and let their belts out. Not Heffenreffer.

It had never been Kate's intention to speak to Heffenreffer, or even to declare her, Kate's, presence. Leaving the session while everyone was involved in defenses of Pulci as a comic rather than an historical writer, Kate made her way back to her room, where the spread had been replaced, stretched out on the bed with several pillows behind her head, and brooded. Those not passionately devoted to the earlier periods are likely to find them soporific. Kate dozed.

She was awakened in the late afternoon by the telephone. It was Leighton. "Have I got news for you !" she announced.

Kate, who almost never napped, and who therefore woke in the afternoon disoriented, gazed frantically about her. "Where are you?" she asked, just avoiding saying, "Where am I?"

"In the goddamn lobby," Leighton said.

190

"They wouldn't give me your room number, only said they'd ring it. Protecting you from the criminal element, I guess, the ones who don't reach you by letter. Can I come up?" Kate told her the room, and went into the bathroom to splash water in her face.

Leighton turned up looking triumphant, which to Kate boded no good, and threw herself into a chair. "How about offering me some booze?" she said. "I deserve it." Kate stared at her; this was not Leighton's usual way of talking.

"What would you like?" Kate warily said.

"Oh, skip it. I'll let you take me home for dinner and I'll have one of Reed's martinis there. I've bearded your Stan Wyman, that's what I've done, and is he ever straight from central casting. I haven't seen anyone come on that way since my section man at Harvard in some damn literary course. I wonder if he ever makes it, I really do."

"Leighton, what are you talking about?"

"Well, obviously, someone had to find out if your Stan Wyman just floated around these conventions looking for action, or if he really was a professor, or, as I suspected, both of the above. So last night, after you drifted off to bed in that supercilious manner — I must say, I don't think your personality is improved by conventions — I looked around in your study and found the *MLA Directory*, and looked, clever girl that I am, under the Ws. And there he was, professor of English at Hofstra. So I did a little more detective work, and tracked him down. I'll spare you the boring details. He was about as hard to pick up as cat hairs. What gave me the idea, really, was that Sherlock Holmes story where the stepfather pretends to be the fiancé, to keep his stepdaughter from marrying; I pretended to be on the make to keep you from selling your honor dear. I do hope you're pleased, but if you growl, I shan't tell you what I found out."

"You do realize the man might be a rapist. You got yourself into the perfect situation. Really, Leighton. . . ."

"I hate it when you start 'really, Leightoning.' Of course he might be a rapist, but I doubted he would grapple with me in the lobby or dining room. I did not follow him to his private quarters, you can trust me for that. And since I gave him a false name and room number in the Hilton — I told him I was in Spanish, and he told me I was at the Hilton — I don't expect to ever see him again."

"He might figure out you're some connection of mine."

"Do you want to hear what he said, or not?

I'll only tell you if you stop playing the stern aunt of yore."

"I *am* a stern aunt of yore."

"Kate, come off it, okay? If you really want to know, I don't think he's a rapist; I don't even think he gets his little victims into bed; he's just one big come-on, if you want my valuable opinion. In any case, I have no plans to see him again, ever. Could we stop discussing sex, and get down to cases?"

"And what," Kate said, "are the cases?"

"Well, naturally, I couldn't ask him about Heffenreffer without fatally showing my hand, but I did establish who and where he comes from — I know, that wasn't difficult — but also that he's one of these incurable pass makers, complimenters, and general collectors of female pulchritude. That means he may well have come on to Heffenreffer if she's half as gorgeous as he says."

"She is," Kate said. "I've seen her."

"We're both pretty slick operators, if you ask me," Leighton said admiringly. "The only risk I dared take was to mention, in my most childlike tones, that I preferred men who liked older women, and he said he'd met one or two older women he didn't think were half bad, and he wouldn't kick them out of bed. That's how he talks, so help me. I wondered if one of them was you."

Kate ignored this. "Leighton, I really think you have to act less precipitously. I don't want to play the heavy aunt, but you must realize you've shown our hand a little soon. Suppose he establishes the connection between us."

"Suppose he does. Really, Kate, I don't think you're half the detective you're cracked up to be, or else you're slipping. He's never going to see me again, so how can he connect me with you or anyone else? What I've established for you is that he is the sort who might have made a play for Heffenreffer, which means that what he told us was true. I mean, if he'd turned out to be some sweet, schleppy guy who was playing a trick or something, that would have meant something else, don't you see? And," Leighton added with the satisfaction of someone who has covered all possibilities, "if you're thinking that you might need me to tail him and that now he knows me, don't worry. I'm great on disguises, even if one were necessary. My guess is that all women look alike to him, if they're good-looking, and that he never notices them if they're not, which shows you one of the advantages of that condition."

Kate gave up the argument. One had to hand it to Leighton; she had established the sort Stan Wyman was, not that there was ever very much doubt, but people play strange games for strange reasons. None of this explained, of course, how he had got to know of Winifred Ashby, but probably he had put himself in the way of being introduced to her. Or he may have made the whole thing up. But what could have been the point of that? Furthermore, his desire for a library card might have seemed farfetched to some, but not to Kate, who knew very well the lengths to which scholars would go to get a card to a major university library, which is why the major university libraries charged seven hundred dollars or more for a card if one was not otherwise entitled. Kate's ad had roused his memory and suggested a scheme.

"If you're through brooding," Leighton said, "I've got another plan. Now don't veto it sight unseen," she said, as Kate began to speak. "I could perfectly well not have mentioned this one to you either, but — "

"Leighton," Kate interrupted, "if you pull one more caper like that with Stan Wyman, you're fired. And don't tell me Holmes didn't ever fire Watson, because that won't wash."

"I thought you'd take that line, which is why I'm telling you, for gosh sake. You know, Kate, you've gotten awfully irritable;

do you think it could be change of life?"

"It is change of life. I've changed my life to include the next generation in my personal affairs, and I'm sorry."

"That's unkind. Wait till I tell cousin Leo what you said."

"Cousin Leo works all day like a slave piling up billable hours in a corporate law firm. He does not dally around with professors of questionable motives and worse morals."

"My plan," Leighton said, "is to try and get to know Heffenreffer, male. He's not at this convention; I've already checked that out. But if he teaches near here, I could scrape up an acquaintance on any number of excuses. It'd be much harder for you, you know. What with your reputation and eminence, he'd be about to suspect something. But I could just consult him about any number of things, and he'd find me indistinguishable from all the other young women he encounters."

This, Kate realized, was probably true. But what would Leighton be able to learn? That Heffenreffer was or wasn't the Stan Wyman sort; that he was or was not an adulterer, a compulsive fornicator, or the sort of scholar who, having married a gorgeous and brilliant wife, is or isn't content to devote himself to academic matters?

"All right," Kate said, "but on one condition, and I mean it, Leighton. You are not to mention Winifred Ashby to him. I don't want to let him know that anyone even knows of her existence. Can I trust you about that?" And Leighton promised.

Kate had arranged to dine with some friends from the West. She enjoyed the evening, and arrived home rather late to find Reed still at work in his study. Before joining him for a nightcap, she went to her own study and rooted out the photocopies she had made that day at the MLA with Elmira. Sure enough, the 1980 session entitled "Oxford Novelists" carried four names, that of the respondent, and the three presenters of papers: Alina Rosenberg, another whom Kate had never heard of, and Martin Heffenreffer, whose paper was on Robert Graves. Alina had not particularly mentioned him, except as one of the men on the panel little interested in Charlotte Stanton. Had that "little" interest been genuine?

Reed, having fixed them each a whiskey, sat on the arm of her chair and placed his open hand on her head. It was an old gesture of his, and it always seemed, to Kate, that strength and comfort passed from him to her, through her brain and down. She leaned her head back against him after a moment, and mumbled into his chest.

"I can't hear you," he laughed, "but I know what you're asking: 'Why, when life is so good, do I complicate it with these detective pursuits?' And I know the answer. Because a life that does not go out to encounter new experiences when they offer soon becomes routine and tiresome. People who are genuinely involved in life, not just living a routine they've contrived to protect them from disaster, always seem to have more demanded of them than they can easily take on. But complain or not, you know this is what living is; it's not just holding your breath until life settles down. Reed Amhearst's creed for today."

"But what do those who take risks and live on the edge do when they haven't you to come home to?"

"That's a nice question, Kate; I like it. But you know it's perfect nonsense. If we are fortunate, we have friends or spouses who listen and support; if not, we are lonely and cope alone. But I really doubt that, in the end, there is ever anyone to come home to. Home is just a place to put up your feet."

"And what is marriage then, Oh swami?"

"Marriage is like the silent partner in that Dickens novel, only instead of taking the blame, the partner in a marriage supplies the status. I am married, therefore I am a responsible person and a good citizen."

"That's a remarkably cynical definition of marriage."

"It's not far off from Jane Austen's, all the same, if we leave children out of it, which, speaking as ourselves, we must."

"I can't think why you wanted to get married, in that case. Somehow, at the time, I thought you had other reasons."

"Of course I did. I couldn't imagine my life if you were not a part of it. Marriage seemed the best sort of partnership offered, and still does. Now I only know that I like to put up my feet in good company, and yours is the best I know. Did you want to discuss marriage, by the way, or Winifred Ashby?"

"It isn't Winifred, really, it's that Stanton woman. She's like Rebecca, haunting everyone's life, and I don't know if it's going to turn out in the end that she was loved or hated, nasty or nice. Do you think Winifred's rather like the second wife, doomed to live in her shadow?"

"The second wife lived on with her enfeebled husband. Do you think Winifred lives on?"

"Reed, my sweet, what can I think? Is it really possible for a grown woman to disappear clean off the face of the earth, and no one happened to notice except Charlie?"

"The farmers noticed. And you'd be surprised how many grown people vanish and stay vanished. Sometimes they disappear into another life, and never reemerge. Sometimes they're dead. Your Winifred sounds as though her whole life were organized for fading into another life."

"You mean she stayed loose. Not many possessions, no entanglements. Reed," Kate asked after a pause, "how much do you know about Toby? And don't answer by asking how much we know about anyone; you know perfectly well what I mean."

"Marriage might be called the capacity to finish one another's sentences. I suspect it succeeds to the degree that this capacity fails. My sense of Toby is that I would trust him with my life, but if you asked me why, I couldn't say. We all know very little of Toby — less, I mean, than of most people. He's simply Toby, which isn't really simple at all. Do you know, I think I sound like you. Maybe a good marriage is a contagion of observations and sentence structure, while a tired marriage is the recognition of opposing attitudes. I like defining marriage; it's almost as challenging as Scrabble."

"I don't know what to do next, Reed. About this case, I mean," she added, forestalling him. Rapidly, she recounted the day's events.

"Why don't we wait to see what Leighton produces in the course of vamping Heffenreffer, and what you learn at breakfast tomorrow about the young Winifred in Ohio? Maybe Winifred vamped *him*."

"You have vamping on your mind," Kate said.

"It's the sort of thing you don't have to be married to notice," Reed laughed. "And what's more, I'll see you're up with the lark for your exciting breakfast, owl that you are."

Breakfast in the suite of a large, midtown hotel was Kate's idea of madness, but she had to admit that James Fenton, who clearly agreed with her, was at least not likely to be jolly at an early hour. He had ordered juice, coffee, and sweet rolls ("I hope you can eat them; they're all the hotel provides in room service. I'm a toast man myself."), and apologized pleasantly for bringing her out at this hour. "We interview all day, and I'm booked up seeing potential tenured acquisitions at night. We're in one of those departments where everyone is going to retire in about four years, and the administration has finally woken up to the fact. I'm sure it's a universal academic condition, but some places respond to the obvious with a little more speed than others. I'm practically the only member of my generation in the department. But you didn't come here to discuss that."

"We're in the same position," Kate said, accepting coffee. "I suppose everyone is. And none of this is helped by the fact that we lost a whole academic generation when there were no jobs, or everybody thought there were no jobs, which came to exactly the same thing. You were good to make time for me. I'm consumed with interest in Winifred Ashby, and am eager for anything you have to say."

"What a pleasure to have someone hanging on my words other than in hope of employment." James Fenton smiled. "I haven't thought of Winifred in decades and yet, when I was young, she was a very good friend indeed. We were both outcasts in a stinking Ohio town, whose only blessing, I at least can say, was that we found each other. As you've probably noticed, I'm lame." Kate nodded. His limp was very pronounced, causing him to dip largely at each step. Yet his limp did not greatly impede his progress.

"I had polio as a small kid," he went on.

"Therefore, I wasn't a 'boy' in the meaning of that term in darkest Ohio. And if you know anything about Winifred, you know that she wasn't a 'girl' within the same meaning. Oh, I don't mean we weren't each a 'normal' boy and girl, to use my absolutely favorite word: normal. Anyway, we joined ranks, I think, because we both saw ourselves as different from the rest of the town, and proud to be outcasts, if the truth be told. You know, it's funny about kids. Mine are all boys — I have to admit the third was a bit of a disappointment to my wife and me, though in our more confident moments we think we haven't let him know it — and I was ready to make them feel just fine no matter how lousy they were at sports or how much they liked poetry — you can guess the sort of thing. But of course, life being what it is, they're all three little macho bastards, dearly as I love them. My wife says it's just a phase, but I think it's peer pressure. If you limp, however, peer pressure doesn't operate, and I limped. More coffee? I seem to be talking about myself and not Winifred, but I'm sure you can see why." Kate smiled, and held out her cup to be refilled.

"Winifred and I were in the same class, and we both chose to take Latin, which was all but unheard of in that place at that time. We both

203

would have liked to study Greek, or said we would, but that was past praying for. We became friends. Privately, really, because if we were seen together we were kidded. Not that it mattered if we were thought to be each other's 'love interest,' but I think we both felt our friendship was simply demeaned if thought of in the only way they could think of it. I can never read the chapter called "The Red Deeps" in *The Mill on the Floss* without thinking of Winifred and me as Maggie and Philip Wakem, although Winifred never transformed herself from a tomboy to a beauty, and I like to think that I was a little less wimpish than Philip. But we were like that — friends, even into puberty. I don't know what would have happened if we'd stayed friends. My family moved to New England, and after that, I didn't see much of Winifred, though we wrote for a while, and then sort of stopped. I've always wanted to see her again, but the opportunity never arose. I didn't think she was in the academic world. That's why your ad shook me right down to my toes."

"You never saw her at an MLA convention, then?"

"Winifred? Never."

"Can you tell me more about what she was

like in Ohio?" Kate asked. "You've told me a lot already, I see that, but . . ."

"What more can I tell you? We lived together in the middle of a spectrum whose ideal type was at either end; she had no interest in anything girlish, which I daresay she exaggerated, but then, so did the other girls, at that age. And while I in my heart of hearts might have wanted to be a 'regular' boy, that was not in my conscious mind. We lived in a sort of no-man's-land, as though the definitions of *boy* and *girl* had no place for us. And yet, we thought we were the best there was; we were full of pride. What was she like? She could do anything a boy could do, but she had the delicacy not to flaunt this in front of me. Still, it was clear that she wasn't going to claim femininity at the price of ineptitude. Do you know Cather's *My Antonia?* The friendship between Antonia and Jim Burden, whose name is rather like mine, tells you something. But I seem always to be coming back to our relationship, and not describing Winifred. Maybe you could ask me some questions."

"Did she ever talk to you about England? Oxford?"

"Yes. I'd forgotten that. She spent her summers there. She had a friend in England, a boy, of whom I remember feeling jealous. The impression I had was that that was where she belonged; not in Ohio. She was rather like Julien Sorel in *The Red and the Black* in that way: her parents weren't her real parents. It's a common enough fantasy, I know; only in her case it was true."

"Didn't she think of her father as her real father?"

"Maybe. It was more her stepmother and Ohio she was repudiating. She was extremely kind, and obviously lonely, much lonelier than I was, since I did have a better home, or at least, it suited me better. It occurs to me what a misfit Winifred was as a girl then, and how easily she would fit in now, as a child. In my kids' school, the girls' soccer team is as good as the boys', and just as important. That kind of thing."

"Did she ever talk about her aunt, her so-called aunt, Charlotte Stanton?"

"No. I wondered what the connection was when I read your ad. She talked about Oxford, and the colleges, but for the most part I had the impression that England was her secret life, apart from me. We had our being in Ohio. Excuse me a minute," he added, as he got up to answer a knock at the door. Kate, since his back was to her, watched the limp closely. She had forgotten about it during their brief talk, and supposed that everyone else forgot about it also. James Fenton was clearly a successful human being, whatever that meant. Well, it meant he was self-assured and likable, doubtless also accomplished, though Kate didn't know in what. He had been chosen to reshape his department not, she felt certain, because he was the right generation, but because of his personal qualities. He welcomed his colleagues and, as Kate rose to go, introduced her.

"I'm afraid I haven't been as helpful as I might have been," he said to her at the doorway, the others having gone into the room. "Please let me know if you think of any more questions. I'll give you my home number as well my office number; please don't hesitate to call. I'll tell you another odd thing. My wife is nothing at all like Winifred, and yet, talking of Winifred now, I suddenly saw a resemblance. They're neither of them types; they both seem to have invented themselves. What an odd thing to say." But Kate said she did not think it odd at all. "By the way," he called, opening the door again as Kate was walking down the hall. "Did Winifred ever marry?"

"Not that I know of," Kate said. "But I don't know much. Did you think she would marry?"

Jim Fenton shrugged. "It would have to be one unusual guy," he said.

Yes, Kate thought, waiting yet again for the elevators, and the world is hardly full of unusual guys. But Winifred had had two fine childhood friends, Kate thought, and had met another in the farmer Ted; that was three more than many people achieve in a lifetime.

Twelve

New Year's came and went. Kate waited ten days for the new year to settle in, and then called Mary Louise Heffenreffer's college to see if they might meet. Leighton, through the incredible network of the privileged young — certain schools, certain colleges, certain professional schools — had managed to arrange to meet Martin Heffenreffer at a social occasion. Someone knew someone whose wife taught at the same place. A party, Leighton had pointed out to Kate, was best, since one more young woman would not make a particular impression, less even than she might have made as the earnest pursuer of academic advice in his office.

Martin Heffenreffer, however, unlike the terrible Stan Wyman, had made no overwhelming impression one way or the other.

Leighton picked up that his marriage was in trouble; this was apparently common knowledge. But certainly he was not flinging himself at every available woman; quite the contrary, he seemed a quiet type, given to conversation and a male listener, what was more — a rare species, according to Leighton. Leighton thought he had a certain look of infinite sadness about him, but that Kate tended to put down to youthful fantasy: middle-aged men often looked infinitely sad to young women, perhaps because they were. Middle-aged women, on the other hand, with their own reasons for sadness, tended to see the opportunities for middle-aged men rather than their failures. Leighton, when this was pointed out to her, agreed. It was, therefore, altogether unclear where all this left the investigation; no further, clearly, than where it had found it. But Kate didn't like to hurt Leighton's feelings by making much of this. No doubt Watson's rather bumbling reputation had to do with the fact that he was always stumbling about at the periphery. Who was it who had said Watson was a woman?

When Kate called the English department at Mary Louise Heffenreffer's college, however, she was only mildly surprised to hear that Mary Louise was on leave for the year.

She had taken a visiting teaching position for a quarter at the University of California, at Santa Cruz. "California!" Kate all but shouted at the poor secretary on the other end of the phone. But she turned out, as do so many women who work in department offices, to have a sense of humor. "I know," she responded, "we're all still amazed. Professor Heffenreffer didn't seem like the California type. But everyone tries it out, sooner or later. We hope she hates it, of course."

Kate got the address from the woman, and thanked her for her graciousness. "Well," the woman answered, "she's very nice, Professor Heffenreffer, and we all hope she gets tired of lying on beaches out there and comes back soon. Have a nice day."

Kate decided to take this advice to heart, and to call Mary Louise in California. There were two weeks left to Kate's between-semester break. Why not spend some of it in Santa Cruz? She had always wanted to see Carmel, hadn't she? Or was it Big Sur? Really, Kate sounded more like an easterner with every passing day; a condition in grave need of amendment. The overwhelming question was: Ought she to turn up in Santa Cruz and surprise Mary Louise, à la Leighton, or should she call first and ask for an appointment? Only a moment's thought suggested the wisdom of the latter course. Mary Louise might be anywhere; she might have gone to Alaska for her holiday. Kate would telephone.

A call to the English department of the University of California at Santa Cruz established the fact that there was no such thing. Professor Heffenreffer was a visiting lecturer in the history-of-consciousness program. Well, Kate thought, why not? Wasn't that her point about Pulci, that we didn't understand his consciousness? Come to think of it, wasn't that what all French philosophy was about? The history-of-consciousness program, when she was transferred to it, turned out to be at lunch. A pleasant recording asked Kate to call back at one o'clock. At four o'clock, her time, Kate did, thinking, If whole offices in New York closed for lunch, what would happen? Maybe there was something to be said for California after all. The history-of-consciousness program was graciousness itself, offering Mary Louise's home number. Wondering if Mary Louise was home for lunch, Kate called. Another machine answered, asking Kate to leave a message for Mary Louise, or Teddy, or Fanny. Kate hung up before the beep; she could hardly ask Mary Louise to call back a total stranger. This was one of those days.

Nor did it improve markedly at dinner, when Kate told Reed her plan. "Winifred disappeared in England, as far as we know," he pointed out. "Why look for her in California, because some twerp connected her name with a gorgeous woman teaching in the history-of-consciousness program somewhere on the California coast?"

"I admit it isn't shatteringly logical when put like that," Kate said, "but there is some sort of connection, even apart from Stan Wyman."

"Just the sort of connection I find most compelling. If I remember rightly, the gorgeous woman's husband gave a paper on Robert Graves in 1980 in Texas at a session in which someone else who has nothing to do with anything gave a paper on Charlotte Stanton and saw Winifred Ashby."

"What a clearheaded way you have of putting things," Kate said, refilling his wineglass. "Somehow, I didn't think the connecting links were as tenuous as that."

"Why not just admit you want an excuse to visit California? As the secretary at Heffenreffer's college said, all academics have to visit California sooner or later, like Christians to the Holy Land. I was in California once, and found it dreary, though admittedly, the Bay

Area is supposed to be better — better climate, better politics, better scenery."

"Would you like to come?" Kate asked. "Everyone says San Francisco is wonderful. We can have a week scuba diving in wet suits, and eating alfalfa sprouts."

"Very amusing. Law schools are not on as abandoned schedules as the rest of the academic world. They have to meet a certain number of days a year, and still get out in time for the best jobs. Besides, I believe in letting you fly away; you're always glad to get back, and especially obliging, I've noticed."

"If I'm not usually obliging, why do I pay the phone bills, and go to parties for Larry's associates?"

"I didn't say you weren't obliging; I said when you come back you're especially obliging, with fonder heart and all that."

"I don't think law school is improving your disposition," Kate said. "Just for that, I won't send you a postcard of a seal, or a picture of a redwood."

"Yes, you will," Reed said. "And Mary Louise Heffenwhatever will turn out to be at the very center of your search. Your instincts are always right."

"But will she see me?"

"If she refuses," Reed said darkly, "you'll

have to send Leighton to pretend she has developed a passion for obscure fifteenth-century Italians, and their place in the history of consciousness."

"Would you rather she went to law school, like everyone else in my family?" Kate asked.

"To Leighton as Watson forever," Reed said, raising his glass. "Why don't you try Santa Cruz again? Your prime suspect might just be getting home about now."

"She's not a suspect," Kate said. "Is she?"

"You must always suspect everybody. Even Charlie and Toby. Don't forget."

"No," Kate said. "I won't." And she went to make the phone call.

Mary Louise was not just getting home, she was making the children's dinner. Of course, Kate thought, children. They were all living, Biddy explained — "Do call me Biddy, everyone does, even the children" — at one of the colleges, Santa Cruz being divided into separate colleges with separate programs. "It's a bit hard to explain, but it becomes clearer when you see it. I'm in Cowell College, which has apartments for visiting faculty." Kate had taken the precaution of again consulting the colleague who had advised her on Pulci and getting permission to use his name. Biddy was happy to meet with Kate. It appeared that Californians were naturally hospitable, and that those who visited picked up the habit. Kate, however, said she would stay at a motel nearby. "Well, all right," Biddy said, "but remember that 'nearby' is a relative term in California. Two hours there and back for dinner is as nothing."

"I'll rent a car too," Kate said.

Two days later, she picked the car up at the San Francisco airport, and drove out to Santa Cruz. Leighton, leaning more to her research-assistant than her Watson duties, had provided Kate with copies of several recent articles on Santa Cruz, the town. One gathered it had a certain sixties atmosphere, which Kate was far from scorning. Excesses there may have been, but selfishness had not yet been sanctified and called, patriotically, American, nor had consumerism and militarism been declared the chief aims of a democracy. Kate did not really think people changed; but she did think institutions, from religions to governments, shifted in what they condoned as the word of God. His word, in Kate's opinion, was permission to do exactly what served one best. If Santa Cruz had contrived to remain backward in this regard, Kate, for one, was glad. However annoying radicals could be, they at least did not have power on their side.

The campus of Santa Cruz, beautiful though it was in the midst of a huge redwood forest, had clearly been designed with radicals, of the sort who had instigated the Vietnam protests, in mind. There was no central space on the campus, nowhere to meet, to gather, to protest. The separate colleges, each of an individual architectual style, kept themselves to themselves in their shelter of redwoods, rather as though they were estates scattered in a resort area. Kate, who was used to stumbling through open spaces crowded with students celebrating everything from Central American autonomy to the return of spring, felt rather uncomfortably like Daniel Boone, walking through forests and over ravine-traversing bridges.

Having settled in her motel on the borders of the town, Kate had driven up to the campus, past herds of browsing cattle. She had acquired a map, and found Cowell College, having passed it only once. Ordinary enough from the parking lot, its grounds looked over the bay — the sort of view, Biddy explained to Kate, that induced in Californians their notoriously long view of life. Unfortunately or otherwise, as one cared to look at it, the apartments for visiting faculty were viewless and dark, though spacious enough. Kate, accepting a glass of iced tea, admitted her confusion about what clothes to wear in this climate. "First I was cold," she said, "now I'm hot. Is every day like this?"

"Every day," Biddy said. "You start the day in layers, which you remove as it heats up, placing them in the *de rigueur* day pack. It takes a little time to figure it all out."

"Are the children enjoying it here?" Kate asked.

"Oh yes, though they find the school amazing. Everyone is into est, and terribly relaxed. I suppose it's a good thing, but when you come from the East, you have a terrible inclination to tell everyone to shape up."

"And the students?"

"Very good. And a really first-rate faculty; it's an interesting place."

Kate, these opening moves concluded, looked about her with some doubt as to how to proceed. The room itself struck her as oddly paradigmatic of her problem. The sun poured in from the French windows in the back, heating the room so that it was necessary to pull the drapes. The picture windows in the front required drawn curtains for privacy. As a result, of course, the room grew dark, and had to be lit, in the middle of a bright afternoon, by lamps.

It helped that she had immediately liked Biddy; they did not need to circle each other, like domesticated animals of different breeds meeting on neutral turf. Biddy, Kate realized, probably assumed that Kate was looking over Santa Cruz in connection with some job offer, or some hope of changing jobs. She waited courteously for Kate to state the reason for her visit. But Kate, momentarily funking it, asked instead about Pulci. Biddy responded with an account of her newest theories, outlined in her recent MLA paper, which Kate did not say she had heard. "Do you know Winifred Ashby, and why she disappeared?" seemed rather too direct as a question. On the other hand, Winifred was not an easy subject to lead up to delicately. Biddy might not know her at all, and Kate could hardly explain that some awful man had suggested that Winifred had been having an affair with Biddy's husband.

"I'm afraid what I want to ask you is rather awkward," Kate said. "Some time ago — I'll tell you how all this came about if you turn out to be at all interested — I had the opportunity to read the journal of a rather extraordinary woman. I found I liked her, and would like to

219

get to know her, but when I tried to find out where she was, it seemed she had disappeared." Kate paused, but Biddy's face held nothing but genuine, if polite, interest; she was waiting for the point to emerge.

"Somehow," Kate went on, "your name was mentioned, very casually, in connection with her, and I wondered if you could tell me where she is, or indeed, anything about her."

"Certainly, if I can," Biddy said, mystified and smiling.

"Her name is Winifred Ashby," Kate said.

She had been prepared for some reaction — anything from a searching of the memory to an exclamation of recognition, but not for the gasp that came from Biddy; it was close to a howl of pain. "Has something happened to her?" Biddy asked. "Isn't she still on the farm? We haven't been in touch in over a year, perhaps longer, except for an occasional postcard in the beginning which said, oh, just: 'Am fine, lovely cows,' that kind of thing. She's all right, isn't she?"

"I take it you knew her — know her — well?"

"My God, what's happened?" Biddy said, clearly stricken. Kate was appalled at what she had done. Damn, she said to herself, you've been clumsy. "I'm sorry," Kate said aloud. "I'm afraid I've been a bungling fool. Could we agree to tell each other all we know of Winifred Ashby?"

"I don't know," Biddy mumbled. Kate felt her pain. It occurred to her, for the first time since her arrival, that Biddy was indeed wildly attractive, but not in a way that Kate kept noticing, as she did with certain women. She was not, despite Wyman's description, stunningly got up, so that one's eye was caught as at a good performance, nor blatantly sexy; she was simply beautiful in a quiet, almost concealing way, as though, knowing her power to awaken male lust, she had done her best to subdue it. "I don't even know anything about you," Biddy answered. "What do you want, really?"

Biddy knew Winifred Ashby: that was evident. What could Kate lose by telling Biddy the whole story from start to finish, in exchange, it was to be hoped, for Biddy's account? But Kate could scarcely demand Biddy's agreement to such a bargain now. I've bungled it, Kate thought. I've got to trust her with the whole thing, and hope for some return of confidence on her part. What have I to lose? If she has done Winifred harm, what damage can I do with my story? If she wishes Winifred well, I may do a lot of good. She may well warn her husband, but she will now do that in any case, if such is her intention. All this passed rapidly through Kate's mind; in the end, as she was likely to do, Kate came down on the side of truth and trust, not out of principle, but because weaving another web of deception could not, as far as she could see, help anyone, certainly not Winifred.

"Has something happened to Winifred?" Biddy asked again.

"I don't know," Kate said. "No, that's the truth. I don't know. No one seems to know where Winifred is. She's disappeared. Look, I'll tell you the whole story from the beginning, and then you decide whether or not you want to tell me what you know about Winifred. As to who I am, I am the professor I said I was, at the university I named; at the moment, I'm investigating the whereabouts of Winifred, whom I've never met. I told you that. Is there anything else you want to know about me?"

"Do you think Mary Garth ought to have married Farebrother?" Biddy asked. "And why didn't Daniel know he was Jewish? Why didn't he look down?"

"What?" Kate said. She glanced around at the closed-in room, and wondered if she had wandered into some Gothic novel in real life.

"Just answer the questions. They're obvious enough, if you really are a professor of Victorian literature. I'm not really paranoid; just cautious. Life hasn't been easy lately."

"Mary Garth," Kate said, "has never been one of my favorite characters. Frankly, whether she married Fred Vincy or not, she would have had only sons and played the patriarchal woman. It's Eliot's only phony happy ending, in my opinion, not universally held by any means. As to why Daniel never looked down to discover he was circumcised, I don't suppose anyone has answered that, but Steven Marcus has tried, among others. Will that do? I thought you were in comparative Renaissance, by the way."

"My husband started in Victorian, and moved up into modern. I guess you're who you say you are. Have you read *Shirley?*"

"Yes."

"Do you like it?"

"Very much. One of the professors here who used to be a dean wrote a good chapter on it in her book."

"Okay," Biddy said. "You pass. Tell me the story."

Kate, while answering Biddy's simple questions, though not perhaps simple to someone who had not read those novels since college, had been, with the back of her mind, trying to organize her story. She decided to tell it, not as it had revealed itself to her, but perhaps as it had happened.

"Winifred Ashby," Kate said, "may have been at the 1980 meetings of the MLA, in Houston, Texas. I can't be sure she was there, and if she was, it's certainly odd that she would have gone all that way to hear a paper on her honorary aunt, Charlotte Stanton, when she could simply have asked the woman who presented it to send her a copy. The next I know of Winifred was last year, when she went to England with an acquaintance of mine. They went to visit a friend of Winifred's honorary aunt, who has been long dead, and about whom my acquaintance, Charlie, wants to write a biography. Charlie and Winifred visited Sinjin, the aunt's friend, after which Winifred simply disappeared. Perhaps she returned to the United States, but no one has been able to find her. The detective who was hired to trace her discovered a journal she had been writing at the farm where she worked." Kate saw Biddy's head come up, saw her decide not to ask a question.

"The journal," Kate continued with a barely perceptible pause, "was mostly about her childhood visits to England, and her life

224

on the farm. That's all I know, all I can tell you, except that, having read the journal, and heard about Winifred from Charlie, I have grown fascinated with her. I want to find her; at the least, to learn what became of her."

Biddy had, by now, got control of herself. "I still don't see why you've come to me," she said.

That of course, was the question. It was Martin Heffenreffer who had delivered a paper at the 1980 MLA session, Martin Heffenreffer whom Winifred's name had been mentioned in connection with. No, not really, it was Biddy's name Stan Wyman had emphasized. Had that alone led Kate to Santa Cruz? She had had to be honest with Biddy, but only, she now decided, up to a point. It was Biddy's turn.

"Did you know her?" Kate asked. "Let's just say, I think you may have."

Biddy got up and walked about the room. "Why should I tell you anything?" she asked. "Okay, you're who you said you are, but so what? You say you want to find Winifred. I've only your word for it that she's disappeared. Suppose I refuse to talk to you, what then?" She turned to face Kate.

"I haven't any threats ready to hand," Kate said, "and I wouldn't use them if I had. What would be the use? Either you want to find out what happened to Winifred or you don't. She's been reported to the police as missing; a private detective named Richard Fothingale has spent many months in search of her. My friends Charlie and Toby have paid him handsomely; no doubt he'd talk to you, if you wanted to pay for his time. Sinjin left Winifred half her money, which was also Stanton's, so the lawyers here and in England know they can't find Winifred. If you don't find all that convincing, why don't you follow the same trail we've all followed? Then, many dollars and weeks later, you might decide to talk to me. On the other hand, as I quite see, you might have decided to distrust me on sight, and wouldn't tell me the time of day if you were wearing five watches. Life's like that sometimes. I have to say that I rather liked you on sight, but it has occurred to me lately how untrustworthy are first impressions."

Kate had been talking, meaning what she said, but dragging it out to give Biddy time to collect herself. I made her feel trapped, Kate thought; I sprang it on her too fast, and she feels she's walked into a snare.

Biddy was perhaps about to answer, but the door burst open, and children streamed in. Yelling "hi," they followed one another up the stairs. Biddy called to two of them. "Come and be introduced to our guest," she said. "This is Professor Fansler; Teddy and Fanny Heffenreffer." The children came up and offered Kate a hand each. "How do you do?" Kate said.

"All right," Biddy said, "you can go now. Try to keep the noise down; we're talking." She then turned to Kate. "Can I get you something to drink?" she asked. "More iced tea?" Kate accepted the offer. They were back to formalities.

Sipping her iced tea, which at least allowed her decently to remain for a few minutes, Kate pondered how to save the situation. It was impossible to ask Biddy to talk about Winifred, even had she been willing, with the children about, running down to the kitchen past the two women. Perhaps in time, a day or two, Biddy would decide to talk to Kate. Kate, meanwhile, might visit San Francisco, or drive down the coast; somehow, neither of these lovely possibilities appealed to her. Sight-seeing, whatever she may have told herself, was not what she had come for.

"Will you have dinner with me?" Kate fially asked. "Tonight, or tomorrow? Or lunch, perhaps ?"

"I'll call you at the motel," Biddy said. "I'll

227

make up my mind and call you. By tomorrow morning, I promise. Leave me the number." And Kate, invited to depart, gave the number and did so. She decided to spend the rest of the day exploring the campus and the town. Disheartened, she got into her car, and drove disconsolately about, trying to arouse herself to some interest in Kresge College, and the others that she had read about in an architectural magazine unearthed for her by Leighton. It was no use; she didn't care. In the end she went back to the town, and simply wandered, finally buying herself a sandwich and eating on a bench on the sidewalk, watching the world go by.

Leighton had talked lightly of a change of life, which Kate did not anticipate for years; the women she knew were into their fifties when this occurred. Was it, anyway, such an important change? It seemed to her that something more profound had shifted in her life: the growing importance of moments like these, moments between events, as at the convention, when with so much to be done, there seemed, at the moment, nothing to do. No doubt people with ordinary, full-time jobs, nine-to-five jobs that often extended, like Leo's and Toby's, at either end, did not suffer this peculiar sense of displacement. I didn't use to find myself at a loose end, no matter where I was, she thought. There was always something to go off and do. But what was there to do here, in this strange place? It was all very well to leap on a plane and arrive on the other edge of the continent because a woman there might have something to tell. But, of course, the woman might not wish to tell it. People did not rearrange their lives to suit one's imperious self. And it occurred to Kate that she and Reed had lives more malleable than most, more able to be rearranged. No, many people their age, their children grown, had the same flexibility, but somehow seemed locked into schedules or self-imposed demands. We are less rooted, Kate thought, more easily distracted, perhaps; more given to investigations, more likely to find time on our hands.

Impatient with these thoughts, she started walking again, ending up, as was inevitable, in a bookstore. The fact that several persons, dressed with an extreme casualness bordering on dishevelment, sat on the floor in the aisles reading books was all to distinguish this bookstore from the many others Kate had browsed in. She bought a novel that had been recommended to her recently, *Tirra Lirra by the River*, by an Australian woman. A quotation from the "Lady of Shalott," who was allowed to see reality only in a mirror or die. There was, it seemed, also a new P. D. James and Kate bought that. With little prospect of sleep, she needed two books at least to hold her for the night. Tomorrow, she would have to decide to sight-see or to say the hell with it.

Returning to her motel, Kate found a message to call Biddy. She did so with her heart pounding, as though she were waiting to hear if she or Reed had a terrible disease or only silly symptoms. Biddy answered the phone graciously enough. "I'll meet you for lunch," she said, "but not in a restaurant. Let's have a picnic in a lovely hidden field I've found on the campus. Let's meet at my house at noon. We can walk from there. I'll bring the food. Perhaps you would bring a bottle of wine and a corkscrew."

To this Kate agreed happily. If Biddy was willing to share a bottle of wine, that must be a good sign. Bread and wine: the symbols of companionship — and of consecration, if it came to that. Kate looked forward to reading her two books on the plane, and fell immediately asleep.

Thirteen

Kate followed Biddy through a wooded path that gave suddenly onto a sunlit meadow. One had the simultaneous sense of seclusion and space. Biddy dropped to the ground and Kate did too, placing her bag with the wine bottle in it next to Biddy's hamper, as though Biddy were the leader in a child's game. First Biddy and then Kate stretched out, shading their eyes with their arms and watching the swallows. Kate thought, This is beauty and peace, but she said nothing; it was up to Biddy to speak. The silence between them was not tense, or limited by impending demands on their time. Kate waited.

When Biddy spoke it was without any of the fear or confrontation of yesterday. Kate was reminded of a novel by E. M. Forster, in which friends at Cambridge met in a kind of dell; the dell had been an image of Charlotte Brontë's also, in *Villette*. Kate did not know if she and Biddy would ever be friends, but they both felt, she was sure, in the presence of friendship, or at the least the possibility of communication.

"They're threatening to build here," Biddy said after some moments. "I suppose it's inevitable. I sometimes think the preservation of space not dedicated to a particular use, impractical space, is one of life's lost causes. Shall we eat, while the meadow lasts?" She smiled at Kate and opened the hamper. Kate extracted her bottle of wine and the corkscrew the man in the wine store had given her. She looked at it and chuckled. Biddy looked up questioningly: as Leighton would have said, the vibes were right.

"That corkscrew reminded me," Kate said, "of a time when I was staying in Cambridge, at Radcliffe. A few of us went on a picnic like this to the Mt. Auburn cemetery — the only meadowlike spaces in Cambridge, reserved for the dead. We had a corkscrew like this, and it broke. One of the women had an umbrella with her — it had looked like rain that morning — and we used the umbrella's tip to push the cork into the bottle. A wine connoisseur would have joined the dead from the shock, but we felt triumphant. This corkscrew, however, seems to work." The cork emerged with a pop; Kate had had to stand up for the task, to grasp the bottle between her knees. She poured the wine into paper cups. They ate and drank in silence, waving away the gnats and feeling the earth beneath them.

"Winifred would have liked this," Biddy at last said. "When I think of her, she's stretched out on grass somewhere, chewing on some long stem she's pulled up, and laughing."

"I wish I had known her," Kate said. "Everything I hear of her is promising."

"It wasn't always summer, of course, or in California; I've never been here before, in fact."

"It sounds like childhood memories," Kate said, "when it's always summer. And for Winifred, I think summer was the best time when she was a child."

"In England, you mean," Biddy said. "There's a beautiful copper beech near where I used to live; very old. It reminded Winifred of one in Oxford. I still don't understand," she added in a different tone, offering Kate another sandwich, "how you came to connect me with her. How did you hear of me at all?"

Kate took the sandwich, and refilled their paper cups. "I heard about you at first from a perfectly awful man named Stan Wyman. Does the name ring a bell?"

"A warning bell," Biddy said, chuckling. "He *is* the most awful man. Particularly awful because, just as you tell yourself that he's not really so bad, he does or says something both frightful and unexpected."

"I know the sort," Kate said. "When I saw him he was just plain awful. I gather he made a play for you that was not well received."

"I tried not to be too off-putting," Biddy said. Kate, looking at her, imagined she had acquired through long experience the delicate nuances of refusal. "Subtlety isn't his long suit," Biddy added. "I don't always say no to everyone," she said, after a pause, as though laying her cards on the table. "Martin and I are separated; we haven't exactly been in great shape for quite a while now. Don't worry," she said, as Kate seemed about to speak, "I'm not confessing for the joy of it. It all has to do with Winifred. Be patient."

Kate, who had been going to say that she meant to probe only so far, nodded. After a time, Biddy spoke again.

"Martin and I weren't getting on very well as far back as seven or eight years ago — something like that, I'm not very good at dates except b.c., before children, and a.d., after disenfranchisement. I figure things out by saying: 'Teddy was two, and Fanny had just been born,' that sort of thing. Martin and I were fine before the children were born, which was almost ten years. Not that we didn't want them; they just changed our lives. We'd decided only to have the one, when I got pregnant again. Probably one of those accidents that wasn't an accident. And once the children were there, and of course I kept on teaching, my life shifted. They became my personal life. I'm afraid I'm not putting this very clearly. Do you have children?"

Kate shook her head. "I married late," she said.

"Odd things happen to people. I suppose there just wasn't enough attention or energy, or desire, left in my life for Martin. I had the children, about whom I felt intensely; I had never imagined I could enjoy children so much. And then there was my work, because I needed intellectual stimulation too. Sorry, I seem to be putting this stupidly, as though it were a prescription for the good life in one of those 'how to live' books, which clearly it isn't. It was fine for me, but there didn't seem to be anything left for Martin. Oh, he was eager enough for sex, but I wanted conversation. And if he was really passionate, I wanted to get it over as fast as possible and go to sleep, as I knew he would. Can you possibly understand all this?"

"Easily," Kate said, thinking: So Martin found Winifred.

"I suppose Martin was bound to find another woman," Biddy went on, as though she had heard Kate. "After a while, it became clear enough he had, and here's the awful part: I was glad. Well, not glad exactly, but relieved, like those Victorian women who were afraid of getting pregnant yet again, and were glad when their husbands shifted to other objects of desire. If anyone had told me b.c. that I would have felt inadequate to male desire, I would have hooted. But I had found a life which suited me: my profession, the children. Not that I wanted to break up the marriage. We worked well together at our life, keeping it — the house, the car, the finances — going. Martin is a good father; he was devoted to the children, and they needed him. On weekends, he spent almost all the time with them. It was a fine arrangement, as far as I was concerned. I think Martin thought I didn't know there was anyone else, and we didn't discuss it. One of the odd advantages of men not going in for long, confidential conversations is that you can get away without discussing things, and they don't mind; they may not even notice.

"Anyway," Biddy went on, "I had what I wanted. Maybe, I thought, the other woman has what she wants. I found Martin and I quarreled a great deal less, as though we were both trying harder to keep our relationship on an even keel. It's odd, isn't it, how no one ever talks about this sort of thing? I've since discovered it's not uncommon, but I thought we were unique."

"That's the way with women," Kate said. "We're separated each into her own home, each feeling a monster if she isn't happy every minute with the company of her small children and her microwave oven. Women need to talk to each other — sometimes, I think it's more important than the ERA — talk to each other honestly, discover we're none of us unique monsters."

Biddy smiled. "We haven't got to Winifred yet; I realize that."

"Am I wrong in guessing that Winifred was the other woman?"

"I suppose that's obvious enough. She met Martin at some sort of miniconference somewhere on Charlotte Stanton; his contribution was the connection with Graves and the other men who were at Oxford after the First World

War. I admit to having been surprised, when I first met her. She wasn't at all what I would have guessed. Somehow, one always pictures men going for much younger, sexier women, though I suppose that's just one more idea we pick up from soap operas."

"For certain men, it's probably true. Stan Wyman, I'd guess, and that congressman, the Fundamentalist who turned out to be sleeping with a sixteen-year-old pagegirl. Certainly we've all been trained enough to conventionality not to spot Winifred as someone's dalliance."

"Anyway," Biddy said, "Winifred went to Houston in 1980 to be with Martin. It was the ideal opportunity. She could say she was going to hear the paper on Stanton in the same session as his. I wasn't going. They would be miles from home and free to have a fine and carefree week. I remember Martin said he was staying on to visit the university at Austin, which had papers he needed to see. I was at home with the children, living the sort of life we manage when he's away: none of us has a schedule; we live easily, spontaneously, without routine."

Kate took a piece of fruit, and refilled their cups. She stood for a moment, stretching her legs, and then sat down again. "When did you meet Winifred?" she asked.

Biddy sipped her wine. "You can't imagine the relief," she said, "talking about this, and to someone who seems to understand. I'm sorry I was so defensive yesterday; you rather took me by surprise. I'd always thought of Winifred as there, wherever she was, as being; it was such a shock to hear she'd disappeared."

"I put the whole thing badly," Kate said. "Never mind; we've made up for it. Now, if we can only find Winifred. . . ." She let the sentence trail off. "Go on with your story."

"There isn't terribly much more. I met Winifred entirely by accident, crossed wires; we both turned up at the same lecture. An English Renaissance scholar was speaking in New York, and I badly wanted to hear her. Winifred went because she'd been a woman Charlotte Stanton had known, and either Winifred meant to meet her at the end or just wanted from nostalgia to hear an Oxford accent. Believe it or not, we sat next to each other. Oh, I know, truth is stranger than fiction, that sort of thing; but it really wasn't all that unlikely when you thought about it. Most of the seats were taken early, and we both arrived late and were let into a section they opened at the last minute.

"We smiled at each other, and at the end of the talk and during the question period, we chatted. I asked her if she'd like to have a cup of coffee with me before I headed back home. Most of the people at the talk seemed to have come with someone, and we were glad to leave together and continue our conversation about English scholars. At some point, of course, probably on our way to the coffee shop, we introduced ourselves. When I said my name was Biddy Heffenreffer, it must have been a god-awful shock for her, though I noticed nothing at the time. After we'd ordered, she asked me if I was married, and I said yes, to Martin Heffenreffer."

"She must have felt like someone in a movie from the 1930s," Kate said.

"Later, when we talked about it, she said hers was the role that should have been played by Bette Davis. Like me, she'd gone to the movies a great deal in her youth, and not much afterward. The children come home with names now I've never heard of, and I think: There's a difference. My parents had certainly heard of Bette Davis. Movies are much more generational now."

"Speaking of generations, you didn't decide to keep your own name?" Kate asked.

"I guess I was just a bit early for that. I wish

now I had. For one thing, with Martin and me in the same profession, it would have been much better. I wonder how long it would have taken Winifred and me to find out the truth, in that case. Because, you see, we liked each other from the beginning. It's odd, really; neither of us had many friends — women friends, I mean — who were interested in ideas and in reconsidering the set boundaries of women's lives.

"Well, of course, Winifred didn't try to get in touch with me. But I knew nothing of her connection with Martin. I was lonely for women friends — most of the women in my community were fine, but they weren't like me; they didn't explore in the same way, they accepted what they were told, and they chatted too much about domestic details. I called her. She'd given me her phone number when I asked her for it; she couldn't think of a good reason not to. Later, we talked about how she felt at that time. The odd part was, of course, that she was so worried about how I would feel, she never even considered the zaniness of her own situation, except that she was getting to care very much about two people who were married to each other. In the end, she took the only way out for a Winifred: she told me the truth. By then, we'd met quite a few times, and I'd offered to read something she was writing, and she listened to my academic woes, and supported me, and cheered me on. Perhaps you understand how important the relationship was to me; not many people would, I expect."

"That's because they're too young," Kate said. "The scarcity of women friends — I mean friends who were out in the world and had more to talk of than recipes and toilet training and what to wear — well, that's known only by the few of us who had only male friends in those days. Women who are always sneering at the woman's movement don't seem to mind having only male friends, or perhaps they take the women friends who came along in the seventies for granted. The shift from a male-centered life to a life where love for men was still possible but not exclusive — who speaks of that? Yes, I can imagine what it meant to meet Winifred. But how did she cope?"

Biddy laughed. "It's so easily said: she learned to accept it. It took nearly forever, but in the end she did. Because she couldn't doubt what I wanted, or what Martin wanted, of course, or what she wanted. I know sharing a man is supposed to be impossible, unless one is in a harem. All the fairy stories, all the old tales tell us that. But I think they're stories made up by men, or meaning something else. Martin and I were good parents, we were good at marriage, however funny that must seem to most people. Winifred wanted a part-time man; she wasn't interested at all in domesticity, or children, or cooking or sewing or interior decoration or even in gardens. She liked sleeping with a man, and exploring strange places with him, and waking up to find him gone and knowing the whole day was her own. The point was, I guess, most people could see it working out just fine. What made it seem eccentric, if not unhealthy, was that Winifred and I became friends."

"Did you talk about Martin?" Kate asked.

"From time to time; if he seemed unwell, or worried, or, as did happen, Winifred had heard some concern he had about the children, we might mention it. I often think how few people have ever written well about friendship, let alone friendship between women. Here's an odd factor about it. Most people one likes, one sees intermittently; one catches up, one talks about the major changes. But because Winifred and I met regularly — every other Tuesday night, as it happens — when I had a regular sitter, and Martin had a regular seminar meeting on modernism, I found that I lived my life in anticipation of those meetings, almost as though I were keeping a journal. One not only lived life, one inscribed it, got it into form for Winifred. And the knowledge that we would see each other, and be able to talk something out, made it more bearable; one was able to sustain oneself.

"One of the odd things I noticed," Biddy added, after a pause, "was that we didn't tell each other the stories of our lives straight off. We didn't bother with anecdotes about the past, the way people do who are mainly happy to find a new audience for the experiences they've already processed. Our pasts emerged bit by bit, but only because we reconsidered them. I remember the first time Winifred mentioned England. 'I never knew you spent a long time in England,' I said. 'Oh,' she said, 'I guess it never came up before.' " Biddy sat up and laughed at Kate. "What am I jabbering on about?" she said.

"About friendship," Kate told her. "We women, I mean — are beginning to tell each other about things, and we have to find the language; it's not always easy, the words having been overused for other purposes."

"Shall we walk?" Biddy asked, turning the wine bottle upside down and shaking it, to mark the end of their picnic. They gathered the remains together and stuffed them into the hamper; Kate put the empty bottle and the cups and corkscrew back in the bag. "There's a nice walk this way," Biddy said, "with a view of the bay when you arrive. Okay?" They set off.

It was necessary to walk single file, and talk was therefore desultory. They both thought over what had been said and heard. Kate thought: They discovered a friendship, and lost it. How? With the view of the bay achieved, Kate might hear the end of it. If it was the end. Biddy stopped by a refuse can, and Kate dropped her bag into it. "The view's just ahead," Biddy called encouragingly.

The view, when they got to it, was beautiful but very far away. The ocean was not nearby, as Kate had somehow expected from the other coast, but distant, beyond the land. "To get close to the sea, you have to walk near the shore," Biddy said. "Down in Santa Cruz, be-yond the town, you can see seals sometimes on a rock, and the water is full of divers in wet suits who look like seals just at first, at least to an eastern eye." They sat side-by-side with their knees drawn up, looking outward.

"Martin found out?" Kate asked.

Biddy sighed. "I suppose it was inevitable.

245

After a time, Winifred tried to break up with him. She still liked him as much as ever, but I think she felt duplicitous, dishonest. And she had to keep watching herself not to mention something about me or the kids he hadn't told her. But I persuaded her to keep on with everything the way it was. She wouldn't have been particularly bothered if we hadn't met. What bothered her was that it was a situation there weren't any stories about; we didn't have any rules to go by; it was a new game. Of course, there we are again. I haven't got the right language for it, and I didn't then either. Besides, Martin was really attached to Winifred. I think it's greatly to his credit that he appreciated her and knew what she was worth, that he loved her."

"Well," Kate said, "there can't be many women who would be wholly satisfied with the situation Martin offered. She wasn't asking for any more, and didn't seem about to. Sorry if that sounds cynical."

"You're right; still, Martin isn't Stan Wyman, which it's just as well to know. I'm shocked often at how many of my male colleagues are on the make."

"Agreed," Kate said, "but I've noticed as a general rule married men either screw around or they don't. Most of them belong to one side

246

or the other. My niece Leighton, I ought to say, doesn't think Stan Wyman is a very successful fornicator, but he's still on the side of those who try."

"Is your niece one of his students?"

"Not exactly; I'll tell you about Leighton later. If you didn't tell Martin, and Winifred didn't, what happened?"

"He saw me and Winifred together. It was god-awful. I'm sure if I ever drown, I'll just keep living that moment over and over, and never get any further back. I ought to say that Winifred at that time was living in a sort of cabin in New Jersey, near the New York line. It was on someone's property, and they rented it to her very cheap. She was trying to write, and didn't need a job to support herself just then. She got some legacy — I don't know if you know about that. . . ."

"Cyril's mother must have died," Kate said.

"Whatever it was, Winifred had saved up some money from the odd jobs she took, and now with this small income she was able to live there in the cabin. We used to meet on one side or the other of the Tappan Zee Bridge for our biweekly dinners. I think she rather missed the structure that a job, even a dull one, gave to her day, but she was determined to try to live without a routine, as she said. She saw Martin several afternoons or nights a week; it wasn't a bad life. Winifred liked to be alone. She said her aunt used to tell her that most full lives are filled with empty gestures.

"Martin went up to the state university at Purchase one afternoon, to give a talk, and on his way back he stopped in at the restaurant where we were; he'd met an old acquaintance, and decided to skip his regular Tuesday seminar on modernism. Somehow, I see it always through his eyes: he looked up, and there Winifred and I were, talking and laughing, clearly deep into a longtime relationship. There are things you can tell at a glance, and sometimes you're right. He didn't say anything. He just stood and looked at us, and walked out of the restaurant. His friend ran out after him, and then rushed back in to pay the bill. It was quite a moment."

Kate looked out over the bay. "What happened then?" she said. "I mean, in the following days."

"Martin couldn't find Winifred. She didn't go back to her cabin, and he didn't know where else to look. It turned out she'd simply checked into a motel, and waited till she knew

he was teaching to clear out of the cabin altogether. It was then, I guess, that she moved to
New England, where she lived in a sort of
boardinghouse, and eventually got the job on
the farm. You know about that; that's where
you found her journal, you or the detective."
Biddy waited a bit. Then she went on.

"Martin went crazy when he got home. As
though I'd betrayed him with fifty men, all
laid end-to-end as Dorothy Parker said. Martin used to be jealous of me; I attracted men,
and it took him a while to come to terms with
that. And I did sleep with someone else once,
and made the fatal mistake of telling him.
That was in the days when I thought honesty
was another word for shifting guilt. He'd been
horribly hurt, but not as bad as this. Or perhaps it's only fair to say the old wound
reopened with this new one. I couldn't seem
to make him see sense. I said I knew it was
odd, but we hadn't planned it, it just happened that way, and hadn't he been glad
enough the way it worked out? In the end he
said he wasn't going to see Winifred anymore,
and we tried to take up our life, but we
couldn't. All the parts of our life together that
had worked so well didn't anymore. We kept
arguing, and hurting each other, and the children took it all very badly. So in the end we

separated. He's told me he's got someone new. I guess that's the end of that."

"Are you thinking of moving here to California?"

"I was. That's why I came here as a visiting professor. But Martin just wrote me and said he would fight for custody if I took the children so far away. So I think I'll have to go back. He's said I can have the house. He's hoping to get another job nearby, but who knows if that will work out?"

"And you haven't heard from Winifred in how long?" Kate asked.

"Close to two years, I guess; maybe a little less. That's how she wanted it; another reason I came to California. She wrote: 'I've got a good job on a farm and am moving into a house they have. Let me try the farm bit awhile, and when I get a sense of where I am, I'll be in touch.' The friendship just wasn't possible anymore, not for a while. Our whole relationship had been transformed. I find it ironic, to say the least, that it worked fine when we were both making Martin happy, and that we lost it when he'd lost his love for both of us; it makes you feel men really are inevitably the center of women's lives."

"With all this going on, I guess it's no wonder neither of you responded to my ad. It must have been a shock to you or Martin if you saw it."

"I didn't see it," Biddy said. "Where was it? Was it about Winifred?"

"It was in the *MLA Newsletter* with her name in big letters and it asked anyone who knew anything about her or Charlotte Stanton to get in touch with me."

"Well, I never even looked at the *Newsletter*. Maybe Martin saw it and wafted it away. We have — had — a joint membership. I expect it must have rocked him if he did see it, but I was too busy trying to keep my life together to read much of anything. I take it none of all these efforts have given you a clue about what happened to Winifred. Will you promise to keep me up-to-date on whatever you find?"

"That's easy to promise," Kate said. "The question is, what will I ever find and when? The list of people who don't know where Winifred is seems to include everyone she's ever met. Have you thought of that?"

"How did you ever connect her with Martin or Stan Wyman or any of us?" Biddy asked.

"I found a piece of plastic with a pin on it," Kate said, "and I didn't know what it was. She registered for the MLA convention in Houston, of course, and wore her name tag in it.

Probably she didn't wear it all the time —
Alina Rosenberg didn't remember seeing it —
but she had it to show when she wanted to get
in somewhere, when she was asked for it. It
wouldn't have been like Winifred to crash."

"She kept her name tag?"

"No. Just the piece of plastic. Maybe she
thought it would come in handy. Maybe she
failed to notice it. Without it, we wouldn't
have met. I hope you do come back east,"
Kate said, as they turned their backs on the
view and walked away.

"The children will be home about now,"
Biddy said.

Fourteen

Kate returned to New York and to her university; the winter settled in, and the semester drew toward midterm before, as it always seemed to Kate, it had really begun. Winifred continued to haunt her, but to no greater purpose than before. Kate, after brooding for weeks, as was her habit, suddenly decided to clear her head by reviewing it all under Reed's baleful eye. She had, upon returning from California, mentioned this detail and that. But, as Reed had learned long ago — soon after he had met her, in fact — questions before she was properly organized in her own mind were wasted on Kate. What manifested itself as a reluctance to answer questions was really a recognition that she did not begin to have the answers.

It was in the middle of a committee meeting

as one of the men was speaking, and he suddenly reminded her of Stan Wyman — so vividly, in fact, she wondered if she was having a hallucination — that something, as she later said to Reed, clicked into place. After a moment, her mind cleared, and she was back in the midst of a salacious anecdote about a distinguished professor whom they could hire, but didn't want to, who had expressed interest in the position but not seriously. "Kate?" the chairperson asked her. "Should we test the waters?"

"Ask him on the phone how serious he is," she said. They were repeating lines as though from a play. Different players said the lines at different times, but it was all in the script nonetheless. The secret of good committee work is knowing when to wake up. It is a narrow line, and many aging professors slip dangerously over it into somnambulation and vagueness. In this case, they were confirming what they all already knew and had agreed to. Kate used to think such meetings a waste of time, but she had learned their value: to expect every committee meeting to be productive, or to expect every conversation to be meaningful, is to leave no space for the routine out of which meaning grows. At the same time, routine, like cocaine, can become addictive, whatever the pundits say, and slowly crowd out life. I am turning philosophical, Kate thought, an indication that I am ready for consultation. But to what purpose?

When she returned home, Reed was mixing a martini, always a good sign. Conversation rather than office work was anticipated. Kate gratefully accepted her martini, and stretched out on the couch. "Sometimes I think we should get a dog," she said. "Imagine being able to come home and pound a large creature whose tail would be madly wagging. Couldn't we get some huge dog, and hire someone to walk it during the day?"

"Whenever you return to a long-familiar discussion, to which the answer is already foreordained, I know you have something on your mind," Reed said. "Can I help? About Winifred, he wisely guesses, being a man who knows you well."

"Do you think the sign of a happy marriage is the knowledge of when the other is ready to talk?"

"I think it's more the sign of friendship, to be honest. Occasionally, married people are friends."

"Interesting how many friends Winifred had; yet when I first read her journal, and she says, after coming to the farm, 'I had found a friend,' I thought: A friendless person. But there has been one friend after another; Winifred had a gift for friendship from the start."

"And not one of them knows where she is."

"Just what I said, Reed, in California. Do you think it's true about great minds ?"

"I think it's true that we may not know of all her friends. Because you have unearthed them does not make them the only members of a fairly exclusive club."

"But I have to deal with what I know about."

"Admitted. But there are huge gaps in Winifred's life about which you know nothing. We don't really know whom she saw when she was working on the farm; because she mentions no one not already in your cast of characters, you assume there was no one. I'm afraid that may be the problem, Kate. This isn't a puzzle in which you've been guaranteed by the manufacturer to have all the pieces."

"But if I put together what I've got, I may be able to see at least where the missing pieces ought to go. If it's just a hunk of sky, why worry?"

"One uses metaphors with you to one's peril; that's something I haven't properly learned after years of marriage. That's because you're a literary type."

"And because everything is a story; one has only to discover what story one is in."

"And suppose it's a new story, never before told?"

"That's what's worrying me," Kate said. "For one thing, we have a friendship between women, each involved with the same man, and not acting like Cinderella's stepsisters. There's a new story for you."

"It sounds fascinating; am I to hear in orderly sequence what in the world you're talking about?"

"Have you got all night?" Kate asked.

"What about dinner?"

"Well, if you'd rather eat than listen. . . ."

"Let's say, I'd like to eat *and* listen."

"It will be like that wonderful movie, *My Dinner with Andre*, where they certainly didn't eat much."

"If you plan only to tell me how you went off to swallow sand on the Sahara with a Japanese monk, I shall have nothing further to do with you."

"I ate fruit and looked at a bay, and watched sunlight through the leaves in a meadow."

"Sounds better already. Let's have another martini, and we'll wander out to a restaurant at some convenient moment, when you pause for breath."

"Reed, are you certain I never bore you with these tales?"

"It is the only certain thing in an uncertain life," Reed said. "I never know what you're going to say, except that it will be amazing."

"I think I'll have two olives in this one," Kate said.

Kate and Reed finished up their discussion of the elusive Winifred in the restaurant over their coffee. (As far as they knew, Kate and Reed were the only two people left in the world who still drank martinis and undecaffeinated coffee; when challenged on this eccentricity, they said that while waiting for fashions in diet to shift round, they were convinced that alcohol and caffeine, taken short of excess, were two of the chief blessings awarded humankind. This pomposity usually ended the discussion, as it was designed to do.)

"If you're not careful," Reed said, "you'll find another fall has come round, brother Larry will be giving another party, and Leighton will remark that Winifred has been vanished now for a year."

"It's more than a year," Kate said. "Larry's party was only when I heard she'd vanished. Along with Charlie, if you recall."

"Do you think they'll be Japanese two years in a row?"

"I hardly think so," Kate said. "Probably the ethnic assignment rotates. You'll be able to tell me, of course, when you get home that night."

"Would you rather not have gone, and not have heard of Winifred, not have renewed your acquaintance with Toby?"

"You can never step into the same river twice. Who said that, Saul Bellow?"

"Sarcasm will avail you nothing," Reed said, retrieving his credit card. "Let's go home and have a brandy."

Some weeks later, Kate had a card from Biddy; she had finished her stint at Santa Cruz, and was back in the family house in Putnam County. She would be glad to see Kate again, if Kate had the time. She added her address and phone number.

Kate called soon thereafter, and accepted the invitation she had hoped for to visit Biddy in her home. Although Winifred had been there seldom, if at all, it was where Biddy and Martin Heffenreffer had lived, and seemed more connected to Winifred than a New York restaurant chosen for the cuisine or ambience or convenience. Biddy sent directions, and

Kate drove up on an uncertain and wintry Friday afternoon in early March.

It seemed a good sign that a very large dog greeted Kate as she emerged from her car. She thumped it happily, as she would have liked more often to do, and mentioned her pleasure at the canine greeting to Biddy, who came from the house to greet Kate.

"We're all glad to be back," Biddy said, "but none is as glad as Daffodil. She was boarded out with friends while we were on the West Coast. She's a good girl." Since Daffodil was a very large, black Newfoundland, Kate assumed, while deciding not to ask, that her name had been chosen either despite its irrelevance or for its inappropriateness: it was a nice name.

"Let me show you the house," Biddy said. "I'm really very fond of it, and am glad Martin was nice about it — my keeping it, I mean. We fixed it up together, and added on to it; it's on all different levels," she added, ducking her head, as did Kate, who was tall. "We've fixed up the attic for the kids, of which we're rather proud. Would you like to see that?" Kate said she would, and followed Biddy to the top of the stairs, from where she could see two large rooms filled with the usual children's paraphernalia, a little room with a TV set, and a bathroom. "The children and I could never have afforded all this space anywhere else now. Downstairs," Biddy said, following Kate back down the stairs, "on this level, we have — I have — my bedroom, and here's my study. Martin used to have a study on the next level," she said, going further down, "but he got too cramped and moved to the basement, where he fixed up one room. We haven't done anything with the rest of the cellar yet; we just use part of it as a laundry and storeroom. No sense going down there, unless you've got a thing for cellars. My father has: he says, don't show him any part of the house till he's seen the cellar and seen if there's water there. And here's the living room, and kitchen. Can I get you anything?"

"I'd love some coffee," Kate said.

"Good," Biddy said. "It will only take a minute. Sit down in front of the fire." Kate sat down, thinking how nice fires were, and shouldn't she and Reed get a country place complete with fire-making possibilities, and Daffodil sat down on the floor next to her and Kate thought: A photographer from some magazine about the modern woman is going to appear at any moment. She could hear Biddy grinding coffee beans, and, in vast contentment, told Daffodil how much she admired her.

"I assumed there was no news of Winifred," Biddy said when she entered with the coffee, "since you had promised to pass on any. Do you take milk?"

"No thanks. 'No news' has a more positive ring than is wholly appropriate to my lack of progress in that quarter. How are the children?"

"Fine, thanks. Glad to be back. They're spending the night with friends, by the way, so don't worry about them. We've got plenty of time."

"I shall probably just sit here with Daffodil until you throw me out. Homes like these seem so delicious when visited in this way; yet I know I would be miserable anywhere but in New York. Do you and Daffodil sit in front of the fire when you're alone?"

"Of course not. I only make the fire when someone's coming."

"I wish you weren't a Renaissance specialist," Kate said. "I always feel so ignorant and dismally modern in the company of those in the early periods, though I guess a medievalist would be worse."

"I have picked up a certain amount about modern lit from Martin, if that's any use," Biddy said. "Actually, the real problem of being in an early field is the tendency of modernists to think life was simple then: no anxiety, no questioning of God, a world somehow together and unchallenged."

"Untrue?"

"Untrue. I imagine being human is pretty much the same at all times. And when modernists say, 'But they didn't have nuclear weapons threatening the world,' I say: 'Ah, but they did think the world could end all the same — plagues, tidal waves, eclipses, wars.' It's never a very enlightening conversation."

"One would have thought, however," Kate said, "that it was easier for someone to disappear in the Renaissance than now. It's not supposed to be all that easy to disappear today."

"I've been brooding about that a good deal," Biddy said. "I suppose it's just as easy, especially for someone not looked for on a daily basis."

"I see what you mean. Winifred, as far as we know, was looked for on a daily basis only on that farm."

"Kate," Biddy said, "we've got to do something. You've got to let me help you. I accepted the loss of Winifred when Martin found out about us; we couldn't go on meeting in secret, corresponding like a guilty couple. But now that she doesn't seem to be anywhere, it's a different matter. I can't seem to think about anything else. Oh, I do my work, I live my life, but it's always there, just below the surface."

"I know how you feel, and I never met Winifred or had her as a friend. But do remember, Biddy, that Winifred is very much a rolling stone. I admit it's hardly characteristic of her to let those farmers down, but she may have had powerful reasons. She lived very much a secret life, hidden, not open to scrutiny, not because she had anything to conceal, but because she was a solitary. She may be somewhere, and she may reappear any day now. We might try advertising. I'll have to find something a little broader-based than the *MLA Newsletter*."

When Kate was ready to leave, Biddy and Daffodil accompanied her to the car. Kate, her good-byes said, had already started the engine when Biddy leaned in at the window. "Kate," she said, "tell me the truth. Do you believe in your bones that Winifred is alive?"

Kate stared in front of her for a while. Then she looked at Biddy. "That's not a fair line to ask me to leave on," she said. "But I understand; you want to deal with my answer alone. My bones are giving me one signal, my hopes, my sense of the general decency of the world, another. People aren't just wiped out, whatever happens on the TV."

"You're babbling," Biddy said.

"In my bones I think she's dead," Kate said. "But I don't know why. My bones have been wrong before now." And she drove off.

"Leighton," Kate said, later in the month, "could you go back on the payroll again?"

"With a song in my heart," Leighton said. "I lay down my word processor with thankfulness, and take up my Watson suit."

"You've really got to be careful. Reactivate that connection with Martin Heffenreffer."

"The friend of a friend of a friend?"

"That's the one. But you mustn't be obvious. Even if you have to take a good while to establish a relationship. What I want you to do is find out about Heffenreffer's current love life: is he living with someone, what is she like, what age, how serious is it? But you mustn't just ask. You've got to let it come out as part of a whole string of gossip. Do you think you can do that?"

"And the management is bearing the expense of all this dillydallying, this series of girlish heart-to-hearts?"

"Of course. The same rate, no matter how long it takes."

"Kate, if you wanted to offer me an allowance, why not just do it? First you pay me for reading, then for gossiping. The mind reels at what you may be paying for next."

"This is the most serious thing I've ever asked of you. Don't muff it, Leighton. Use to the highest those instincts that made you ask the students outside my office how they liked my class."

"Still rankling, is it?"

"I use what the Lord offers," Kate said, "and we all know what high quality that is. Leighton, I'm serious."

"You are always serious," Leighton said. "Your marvelous use of persiflage has never fooled me for a moment."

"Well, be careful; take your time."

"At these rates," Leighton said, "I may take forever. Martin Heffenreffer may have carnally known at least fifteen teenyboppers."

"Exactly the information I want," Kate said, waving her away.

The semester ground on. Not that Kate now or ever found it tedious. But she had a sense of letting time pass, not because time would produce anything, but because it did not matter that it passed; meanwhile, as a professional, she had a job to do.

Toward the end of the semester, she sent a

note to Stan Wyman, asking him if he could conveniently meet her at the Faculty Club to talk about the possibilities of his getting a library card. She couldn't say what would be possible on a permanent basis, but he could probably get a card as a postdoctoral fellow under her sponsorship.

Then she made an appointment with Charlie. Kate stopped in again on her way home, as Charlie emerged from her study looking like someone who had just returned from an outing with Pantheus's mother. She kept running her fingers through her hair, accomplishing a perfection of which a punk hairstylist might despair.

"Do you mind if I ask a few repetitive questions?" Kate said. "I'm sure we've been all over this before, but I've emptied out my mind, and have to begin filling it again."

"Kate, have you thought of something?"

"I have thought such things that it were better my mother had not borne me. Anyway, I'm asking the questions. You did trace Winifred's birth certificate?"

"I told you."

"Good; tell me again."

"The child was registered in her father's name. That is, his name was genuine; the mother's was not."

"That's what I'm getting at. How can you be sure of that?"

"Because there's no such person. Mr. Fothingale found a few women of that name, to be sure, but they weren't she: wrong age, clear histories. It was all very obvious."

"Okay. (I've taken to saying 'okay' lately; I think it has to do with the fact that nothing is in this case.) Did you ever check up on Charlotte Stanton's medical history?"

"Her medical history? Not especially. I know what she died of. Kate, you're not suggesting that someone did away with her."

"No, you fool, I'm suggesting that if you can find her medical records, they might indicate if she'd ever had a child. I think doctors can tell if a woman has given birth by the state of something or other. It just struck me as a way of establishing once and for all if Winifred could possibly have been her child."

"Kate, that's brilliant. Why didn't any of us think of that?"

"No doubt because there are no such medical records, no doctor conveniently jotted down the fact in his bloody little notebook. Still, you might try. It sounds exactly up Mr. Fothingale's alley to me, if you can afford to send him back to England. Do you know any-

thing about the going-down plays at Somerville in Stanton's time?"

"The what?"

"The plays the students wrote and per-
formed in their final year. Actually, through
the efforts of Leighton, I came on a reference
to it. It's not important, except that Stanton
was in the leading group who might have put
it on, and I wondered who was in it. Maybe
Fothingale, if he goes, could find out with a
discreet little visit to Somerville. But it's not
really necessary. I'm sure one could do all this
by mail. Or I could send Leighton, except
she's on another assignment just now. Don't
interrupt," she added, as Charlie seemed
about to speak. "My thoughts keep escaping
me; perhaps it's age, but I think it's despera-
tion to get the unconnected facts, if you can
call them facts, into some kind of order. Next
question: I want to know all the ins and outs
of English citizens making wills in this country: Why do they do it if the heir is American?
Has it some connection with taxes, or with in-
ternational exchange, or nothing to do with
anything? Also — well, I better ask Toby that
one. Back to the Harvard Club, I can feel it
coming. Well, so long, Charlie. See you."

"You aren't *going!*"

"That was the idea."

"But you haven't told me what all this is about."

"When I discover what it's about," Kate said, putting on her coat and gathering up her belongings, "you shall be among the first to know. An event which in all likelihood will never take place. Bye."

No one seeing Kate at this time would have had the smallest inclination to compare her to Sherlock Holmes.

Two weeks later, Stan Wyman turned up at the Faculty Club, where Kate bought him a drink. "Nice place," he said, stretching out his long legs. Kate had no intention of wasting time by challenging that observation.

Stan Wyman was well into his third drink when Kate asked the question she had been mulling over for months. She led up to it in what she hoped was a mildly flirtatious manner. "We might never have met," she said, "if I hadn't put that ad into the *MLA Newsletter*, and you hadn't happened to know about Martin Heffenreffer's relationship with Winifred Ashby."

"Now, don't get me wrong," Stan said. "I didn't exactly say it was a relationship. All I said was, Martin Heffenreffer was seeing someone, and she happened to be the one you were advertising about. I never asked you why, by the way."

"What do you mean by 'seeing'?" Kate asked, skipping over, she hoped forever, his last question.

"Oh, for God's sake. I just mean they were having a drink and an intense conversation, the way men do with women if they're really turned on. I only took note of it because Biddy Heffenreffer had made such a point of how hers was a devoted marriage, neither of them ever wandered further than the corner grocery; I didn't really believe her, and here was proof I was right."

"How did you know it was Winifred Ashby?"

"I didn't, of course. I went up to Heffenreffer just to have a private gloat. I held out my hand to her and said, 'Hi, I'm Stan Wyman,' so of course she had to shake my hand and tell me her name. I admit it kind of stuck in my mind for future use, but I haven't seen Biddy again, worse luck, and I might have forgotten all about it but for your ad."

"And my ad might have led to a faculty card?" Kate said. Stan nodded. And to the kind of intrigue you batten on, Kate thought but did not say.

"Now, about that card?" Stan said, waving his empty glass.

"Do fetch yourself another drink," Kate said. "And, about the card, you apply to the dean for a postdoctoral fellowship, and I'll write supporting it. Here's his name and address." And may the university forgive me, she silently added.

"Can I get you anything more?" Stan asked.

"No thanks," Kate said. And then, as he walked off toward the bar, she stopped him for a moment. "Where was it that you met them," she asked, "Martin and Winifred?"

"The airport," Stan said. "I was off to visit my old ma in Colorado. I don't know where they were going. Hold on just a moment," he said, waving his glass.

Kate felt ready to wait forever.

Fifteen

By the end of the semester, some answers had come in, none of them mind shattering. In fact, they were all either negative or expected, as Kate complained to Reed. Leighton had discovered with much less trouble than Kate had anticipated, and without arousing the slightest suspicions in anyone — gossip was gossip, and would ever be, and where would we be without it? — that Martin Heffenreffer had been involved for the last year or so with a young woman not easily identifiable — she wasn't a student or in any way in the academic world, nor any other kind of professional. All Leighton could report was that she was rumored to have been the girl friend of some Mafia type, but Kate decided to take the general impression for the fact. One knew, at least, what sort she seemed to be.

Charlie, using a transatlantic reference from Mr. Fothingale, had had a search made for Charlotte Stanton's medical records. Oddly enough, this turned out to be ridiculously easy. Stanton had had a gall-bladder operation during her term as principal of her college, and the hospital records were still available at the nursing home. They included, in addition to her other medical history, the fact that she had never been parturient, which seemed to settle that.

"But she might have lied to the question. I mean, they might just have asked her, or whoever examined her may have been wrong," Charlie, a last-ditcher by nature, said when she heard this. Charlie believed Stanton was Winifred's mother, and would, Kate suspected, go on secretly believing it forever.

And, it had transpired, Stanton had taken part in the going-down play her year at Somerville, and guess what: Sinjin had been in it too; they had written it together. Really, Charlie said, Kate was clever, though of course she, Charlie, when she went to England for further research, would have found all that out. Kate said she had never doubted it, but just happened to be wondering now. "And what Somerville can have made of a detective inquiring about going-down plays, I can't imagine," Charlie had added. Kate merely supposed that Stanton's fame, to say nothing of other well-known graduates, must have long since inured them to this sort of thing.

Toby, glad to have lunch again with Kate, had been happily vague about the will. "It was a sensible thing to do, if you knew the heir was an American citizen, living in the States."

"But in the first will, Stanton's, her heir was Sinjin, who wasn't an American citizen and wasn't living in the States."

"But that was different. She became terribly ill here, and like many people hadn't made a will in years. She probably thought she had heart trouble; maybe it was just that gall-bladder condition Charlie found out about. That was clever of you, by the way."

"How are you, Toby?" Kate had asked.

"Never better. Charlie and I are going to get married, and we can tell everyone all about it. They'll give us a party; it will really be quite an event. By the way, I haven't seen much of Leighton lately. Has she given up word processing?"

"Temporarily," Kate had said. She was glad about Toby.

The evening Kate picked on which to expound her theory about Winifred and her friends happened to be the day of her university's commencement exercises. Kate attended them perforce, having been tapped to be a marshal. This happened about once every five years, and always gave Kate a secret pleasure, though she would have died rather than admit it. She didn't walk in the procession, but stood with the groups of graduates she would be shepherding to their section of seats, watching the procession and thinking this ceremony had a grip on one's emotions that was beyond explanation. The fact that all the participants were roasting in long robes and hats on a sunny day added to the illogic of the whole event. Ours is no longer an age for such ceremonies, as the undignified antics of some of the students clearly suggested; but they, like Kate, were moved nonetheless.

Kate had recently learned something about commencements around the country that amused her. Moved though she may have been, she went only when conscripted, and then complainingly. Most faculty members did not attend at all, leaving the academic procession meager, and a disappointment especially for the parents, who had invested in the neighborhood of fifty thousand dollars for the degree about to be bestowed upon their progeny. In recent years, someone had told Kate, the colleges and universities had grown tough. Either it was in the new professors' contracts that they had to attend commencement in academic regalia or — this was Kate's favorite ploy — the final check of the academic year was handed out at commencement, and was not mailed for a month to those not there to receive it. *Autres temps, autres moeurs.*

So she returned home tired and hot, but determined to get it all out on the table. She had asked Toby and Charlie and Leighton to join her and Reed for a postprandial confabulation. ("That means she's going to talk all night starting after dinner," Leighton had explained to Leo. She had promised him a report. Kate had said he might come, but one of the senior partners was preparing a brief that, as Leo pointed out to Leighton, would be read, if at all, by the judge's clerk, who was someone who had been in Leo's class at law school. "I could just call her up and tell her the gist in five minutes," Leo had complained. But one is not paid fifty thousand dollars a year by corporate law firms to chat with judges' clerks.)

Kate did not ask Biddy Heffenreffer, though she had talked to her, and requested permission to tell Toby and Charlie and Leighton about Winifred and Martin. Biddy was reluctant, but resigned; she was, after all, intelligent and sensitive enough to have been Winifred's friend. "What have I got to lose? There's nothing to be ashamed of; it's all just a goddamn pity." In which Kate concurred.

"Here's how I see it," she said, when refreshments had been served all around. "What you all have to do is tell me where I went wrong, or why my guesses are all out of line. Because it's all guesses. Let's be clear about that. I don't think we'll ever know the truth about all of it, perhaps not about most of it. But I had to put it together into a story, because I love Winifred; it's that simple. I think she was a remarkable, a wonderful person — how words fail us. Those she befriended never forgot her, always had the sense they had been in the presence of something, if not unique, then rare indeed.

"What we've got, as you all know, are two stories. One, the story of one woman scholar and writer in England who died some years ago, and another who died only recently. That's one story. The other story is American, and has to do with a man Winifred loved, or, at any rate, needed and enjoyed, and had an extended affair with."

They, all except Reed, who had heard it all before, stared at her. "I never thought of Winifred as loving men," Toby said.

"That was one of our mistakes," Kate said, "though less mine than it might have been, I'll say that in my defense. Because she wanted to be a boy when she was young, because she didn't like the usual 'feminine' things, one didn't think of her as a woman likely to become passionately involved with a man. But all it required was the right man. Think of Cyril, the little boy in England. He went on being her companion in the summers, though she hasn't left us the details of those later years. They were separated by — we don't know what; perhaps the exigencies of time and distance. We do know he left her his money. She must have meant more to him than just childish derring-do. Perhaps he guessed at what a mature relation with her might have been like. The man I met at the MLA, who had been her friend in Ohio" — the others looked up, startled, and Kate stopped to explain about James Fenton, and his account of the youthful Winifred. "What I'm trying to say is, despite all the hints to the contrary — James Fenton mentioned that his wife had something in common with Winifred — we thought of her as not a sexual being, at least, not in relation to men. We've all been trained to think so conventionally, neat types in neat round holes.

"What we have to remember is the sort of man Winifred's father was. He was devoted to the child, and kept custody of her, though that was a quite unusual thing to do in those days. He wanted her with him in America. At the same time, obviously, he recognized Stanton's right to her and let her spend the summers at Oxford. We also know that she was living in England until he was able to make a home for her in the United States. So he was unusual not only in his devotion to his small daughter, but also in having loved the sort of woman who was her mother. Because whoever that was, she had to have been known to Stanton; a scholar, an intellectual, a woman not wholly unlike Winifred."

"Charlotte Stanton, in other words," Leighton said. "Why not say so straight out?"

"Because it wasn't Stanton," Kate said. "We've come closer to confirming it with the medical report that she never had a child, but we knew it before. According to Winifred's journal, her 'aunt,' Charlotte Stanton, told Winifred she was not her mother, and that Winifred must believe that whatever others said. Stanton, as I picture her anyway, wouldn't have said that if it wasn't true. That's the kind of lie Winifred couldn't have told, and neither could anyone connected with her. Stanton was helped, of course, by the fact that Winifred didn't really care who her mother was; at least, not consciously enough to pursue the matter. She wasn't in search of a mother; that's rather a recent concept, after all, and what Winifred wanted was a broad world, like that reserved for males, to move in. She didn't want another feminine influence."

"You think it was Sinjin, then?" Charlie asked.

"Yes," Kate said. "That's what I think. It's what makes sense, no matter how you look at it. Sinjin left her money half to Winifred; she wanted to see her, to clear the biography of Stanton with her. She used Charlie to find Winifred; she wanted Winifred's blessing. Stanton may have considered leaving her money to Winifred when she made that will with Toby, but Sinjin had talked her out of it — that's my guess — or she had decided it would be used as evidence of the obvious, and wrong, conclusions.

"I think Sinjin fell in love with Winifred's father. We should be able to find out more about that: we'll leave it for Charlie. We can assume that he served in England during

281

World War II; he must always have had a feeling for England, because he was there before
the United States got into the war. Most im-
portantly, we know he claimed Winifred at
birth. Charlotte Stanton was attached to Sinjin; let's say she loved her — I'm not describing the relationship; I think we know damn
little of the relations between women anyhow
— but when Sinjin got pregnant, Stanton
helped her out. I'm guessing, this is all
guesses, that Stanton took a good bit of time
deciding what to do with her life. In the end,
she chose the academic vocation — the right
one, as it turned out. She was devoted, in her
cool way, to Sinjin's daughter — perhaps she
wanted to adopt her. We'll probably never
know why Winifred didn't go back to England when she was ready for college; some
mundane reason, in all likelihood. When
Stanton came to America, perhaps she saw
Winifred; all we know is she became ill and
made her will. Then she went back."

"It seems to me," Leighton said, "that
you're making this all up from scratch. You
haven't any proof. You're like someone writing a biography who hasn't even looked at the
evidence."

"Let me tell you a story about Sylvia
Plath," Kate said. "A critic has written how,

after studying Plath, she saw how influenced Plath had been by Virigina Woolf's *The Waves*. Later on, she had a chance to go to Smith College and examine the Plath papers. There was Plath's copy of *The Waves* underlined at exactly those points the critic had mentioned. But suppose Plath's copy of *The Waves* had not survived, or not been sold to Smith, where it could be studied? You would have said there was no evidence. I think evidence will be found for much of my story."

"Are you saying," Leighton asked in her most Harvard tones, "that you are treating Winifred's life, and the lives of her antecedents and friends, as though they were a text?"

"I wouldn't put it so grandly," Kate said, "but yes, that is what I'm doing, I suppose. Leighton, dear, do try to recapture the Watson pose, and just make admiring grunts."

Leighton snorted. "But," Toby asked, "where was Winifred before her father came for her? Had Charlotte Stanton, or Sinjin, farmed her out?"

"Oh, yes, I think so," Kate said. "By then Stanton had taken up the academic life. She couldn't keep the child, and Sinjin married and was soon to have George. I think they both realized the father would make the better home for Winifred; they were wrong only in not realizing the sort Winifred was. As we now know, she would have been far happier boarding with Cyril's family and living in Oxford. As I switch over now to the other part of Winifred's story, the later American part, do bear in mind something I forgot, or didn't understand in the right way. Winifred liked her 'aunt,' she liked Charlotte Stanton. The two of them were on the way to being friends, which I think would have become clear had Winifred finished her journal."

"If she'd finished it, we wouldn't have got to read it, and we wouldn't be here talking about her," Leighton pointed out.

"I might have got to know her better," Charlie sadly said. "She might have chosen to show me the journal."

"Anyway," Kate said, "we can certainly conclude from Winifred's having bought the book about her 'aunt,' that she was fond of her; that Charlotte Stanton had appealed to Winifred's imagination." Kate paused a moment.

"The other story," she said, "I feel much less comfortable telling, not only because it's a bad story; it's also about people living now, at this time, and not, like the two English friends and Winifred's father, with their lives behind them, over."

"You ask for discretion and confidentiality, and we offer it," Toby said.

"I've already told you Winifred was having a love affair with a man, a professor of literature named Martin Heffenreffer. Leighton has met him; I have not. Would you care to describe Martin Heffenreffer for us, Leighton?"

Leighton, as Kate had known she would, blew up. "*He* was Winifred's lover! For God's sake, Kate, you might have told me. You especially told me not to mention Winifred's name to him, but you didn't tell me why."

"I didn't know why then," Kate said. "If you'll listen, you'll see that I found all that out later."

"I'm not at all sure Watson listened to Holmes quite this continuously. And Watson got to write up the stories, which I have a horrible feeling I'm not going to be allowed to do."

"No, my pet, you're not, except to the extent that you can help Charlie with her book. I'm sorry, and I'll try to make it up to you. We'll think of something." Leighton snorted, but she was not, Kate knew, really surprised. Leighton had figured it out long since.

"An awful man named Stan Wyman answered my ad in the *MLA Newsletter*, and — "

"Answered your what?" Toby said.

"Maybe you should have written it all out first," Reed said to Kate. "Can I get anyone another drink?" He got up to collect glasses. "Go on," he said to Kate, "I'm listening."

"He isn't," Kate said, "but he's heard it all. Poor Reed. His choice to be here, however. Where was I? Oh, yes." And she told them about the plastic badge holder, and her visit to MLA headquarters, and her reasons for attending this past year's convention, which had been, heaven be thanked, in New York. "I discovered that there had been a paper on Charlotte Stanton at the Houston convention in 1980, and I put an ad in the organization's newsletter to see if I could flush out anyone who'd seen Winifred there. I've told you about the childhood friend from Ohio. Then there was the professor, Alina Rosenberg, who'd given the paper on Stanton. And then there was Stan Wyman, who approached me anonymously, in keeping with his high sense of morality, and told me, while doing a little blackmail on the side, that he'd seen Winifred carrying on with Martin Heffenreffer. By the way, Leighton dear, just as a side remark, let me point out that I deduced five different ways that Winifred had been at Houston, but it only occurred to me a week ago to check with the MLA to see if she'd registered. She had. Simple as that, and what you'd call evidence."

"I can't say I'm exactly clear on all this," Charlie said, "but I'll let it go by and try to bring it into focus later. We have Winifred deep in an affair with Martin Heffenreffer, who (I want to know but am afraid to ask) is married?"

"He was," Kate said. "And this is the very end of my tale; you've all been very patient and long-suffering. Martin's wife is a woman named Mary Louise Heffenreffer, but called Biddy; she was described to me by Stan Wyman as gorgeous, and she is. She's also a professor of Renaissance literature. She and Winifred met quite by accident, though it was bound to happen sooner or later, one way or another. They liked each other, and became close friends: love and friendship, that rare connection between two women. Winifred, of course, told Biddy about Martin, and the two of them found that each had from him what she wanted. It's shocking at first, but not if you think about it for a while, clearing your mind of misconceptions. I know a few women who are 'mistresses,' as they call themselves. They don't want kids, or houses, or laundry; they like seeing a man from time to time, traveling with him, sleeping with him. The wife, meanwhile, has what she wants: children, a father for them, her own sense of herself. No one has ever taken a survey of how many wives are happy when their husbands are away. The only new part here is that the wife and 'mistress' knew each other.

"Eventually," Kate continued, "Martin Heffenreffer found out. Not unexpectedly — "

"Wow," Leighton said. "It must have blown his mind."

"Yes. That's a very good description, as it happens," Kate said. "And he couldn't get his mind back together again. You see, it wasn't just that he found out they knew each other; he found out they were friends, close friends. Winifred faded away, and Martin and Biddy tried to put their life back in place, but there was no chance. They separated, and are now almost divorced. Martin has the children weekends and during vacation; schooltime, they live with Biddy in the old house. The children didn't want to move, or leave their school, and Martin couldn't have got custody anyway."

"I see the problem," Leighton chuckled. "You can hardly say to the court that your wife had befriended your mistress, which proves her an unfit mother."

"He still had his rights," Reed said. "When Biddy mentioned moving with the children to California, he said he would fight it, and he might well have won."

"So what happened to Winifred?" Charlie said. "Did she go on seeing Biddy?"

"No. Winifred sent Biddy a card from the farm, but then Biddy had to agree that they would stay out of touch for a while. Then Biddy went to California, where I saw her. The greatest loss was Biddy's. Winifred must have treasured her new friend, but Winifred was used to solitude; she'd always lived alone. Biddy lost her husband and her friend; looking the way she does, men being what they are, Biddy can always get another husband. I rather think she had come to treasure the friend above all else."

"Well," Leighton said, "I hand it to you. You're a great storyteller. But don't drag it out anymore. Where's Winifred? You know Martin's shacked up with a tootsie, because I found that out for you. I guess he went for a change of pace. Me, I'd have stuck with Winifred. She grows on you."

"I think she had grown on him," Kate said. "Fool that I am, it didn't occur to me for months to wonder when Stan Wyman could have seen Martin and Winifred together. I just assumed he'd seen them some vague time in the past. But when I got my head together and asked him, he said he'd seen them in an airport, not that long ago."

"You mean," Reed, who hadn't heard this part before, said, "you think Martin got Winifred to come back from England and met her plane the day she left that note for Charlie, and no one ever saw her again?"

"Yes," Kate said. "I didn't tell you that part, Reed, because I couldn't face the implications of it. Implications, hell; it's almost a certainty."

"What is?" Leighton said. They all looked stunned.

"That Winifred's dead," Reed said. "She's been dead since before Larry Fansler's party."

Sixteen

"It must have been quite a moment," Reed said when the others had gone and he had brought her a nightcap, "when Stan Wyman told you when and where it was he'd seen Heffenreffer and Winifred."

"It's why I couldn't tell even you."

"It's not like you, Kate, to turn away from a fact."

"You're wrong, Reed, but thanks for the compliment. I practice denial regularly; it's my chief means of coping with everything from physical symptoms to political despair. But sooner or later something seems to harden into fact, and you have to face it. That's where I am now, or think I am. And if I'm right, what did Martin Heffenreffer do with the body?"

"Have you an idea? Let me remind you, it's

not that easy to dispose of a body."

"That's what they say; I've never understood it. Take the farm where Winifred worked; you haven't seen it, but it's surrounded by fields and woods. If you just dug a deep enough grave, and put the body in it, who would notice?"

"It surfaces eventually," Reed said. "Maybe not for years, but that would hardly be security for the man who put it there. Did you know that when someone buries a body in the desert, a flower grows there, nourished by the decaying flesh? A sure giveaway. In the woods, dogs dig bodies up."

"I know, I know," Kate said. "And here in the city, criminals encase the bodies in cement and drop them in the river."

"Have you ever tried working with cement? You need a place to mix it, and a way to dump anything that heavy in the river. That's gang work."

"I think it was cement all the same," Kate said.

"In the basement, I suppose you suppose."

"So you thought of it too?"

"How could one help it, with your tales of unfixed-up basements, and Biddy's telling you the only room down there apart from the laundry was Martin's study? He had only to do the job when she was in California with the kids, taking his time. Then he moves out. Is that more or less how your thoughts were running?"

"Reed, sometimes I think we've been married too long."

"I wasn't reading your mind, my love, I was drawing the logical conclusion, as you were. The question is, what can be done about it?"

"Is it really that easy to dig a hole in a basement floor, and to put a body into cement? I'm trying to think logically, as we should, and not notice we're talking about Winifred."

"It's damn hard," Reed said. "But it could be done, if one had plenty of time, and no likelihood of being interrupted. He'd break the cement floor up with a pickax. He'd mix the cement in any large wooden receptacle, perhaps an old bureau drawer. If it was wooden, he could burn it, leaving, of course, bits of charred cement, but he's not counting on anyone's coming to look for evidence. He'd drop the body into the hole he'd dug, pour cement over it, and level the whole thing off in the end, so that, to the casual eye, what he had was the same cement floor as always. He might, if he was thorough, dirty it so that the new part looked no different from the old."

"All right, suppose he did that," Kate said,

looking as ill as she felt. "What do we do about it? Ask Biddy if we can borrow her house for the weekend, and dig up the basement?"

"Not to be recommended," Reed said, "for a number of reasons. I'll spare you the obvious ones about warrants and destroying property. There's also Biddy. Suppose Martin got a good lawyer who could come close to proving that Biddy had buried her there? I doubt our understanding of the strength of the friendship between the two women would carry much weight in court."

"Obviously," Kate said, "we are going to have to face him with it. That is, I'm going to have to face him with it. If there are two of us, he'll simply shut up. He's got to be enticed into conversation, and then shocked into self-incrimination. And don't try to argue me out of it."

"Certainly not," Reed said. "I think it's a super idea, simply super. You accuse a murderer of his crime, indicating along the way that you know where he buried the body. Then you get up and walk away. Kate, a man who has killed once will kill again to cover the crime. Even if you're willing to risk finding yourself in the basement with Winifred, I'm not."

"But you'd know where I was, and could dig us both up."

"True, there is that consolation. Don't forget that killing you would be worth it to him. You can't be hung for more than one murder. We don't hang people now, thank God, but the principle's the same: in for a penny, in for a pound. Of course, I'm babbling. Kate, I've been wildly supportive of your antics over the years — forgive me: of your very important investigations — but this time you have to listen to me. Unless I'm with you when you confront him, and we have a decent backup system, you cannot risk this. It won't help Winifred, let me point out."

Kate tried hard to speak calmly. "Reed, surely you can see that I can't just sit back and let him get away with murdering her, without at least finding out what happened. And you know enough of the police and the D.A.'s office to know they wouldn't listen to me, or even you, for a minute. *Habeas corpus*, and all that. I know it doesn't mean you need a body, but it does mean you need a case, and all we have is Winifred's disappearance and wild suspicions. You can't argue with me there, can you?"

"Why don't we both talk to him, then?"

"You mean, ask him here for a social evening with an old married couple and just say, an hour after he arrives: 'By the way, where did you put her body?' "

"Why is he any likelier to talk to you if you meet him alone?" Reed asked.

"It's more logical," Kate said. "After all, he used to work in my period. I read his paper on Graves, and I could indicate a new interest in Charlotte Stanton, about whom by now I can sound quite knowledgeable, believe me. He doesn't know I know Biddy, I'm pretty sure of that. There is a chance that he saw my ad, and that would make him suspicious, but he could hardly refuse my invitation on that account; in fact, he'd have to accept it. *My* invitation. Reed, don't you see, I could bring that off, but not if it's a social occasion with me and my significant other. I've got to see him alone; it's the only way I'll manage it at all. You do see; what I love above all is your ability to see things honestly, and admit it."

"How about this, Kate? You get in touch with him, arrange to meet him, but somehow — I don't care with what excuse — get him to meet you here. I won't be in evidence; you can tell him you're alone, or just let him assume it. But I want to be in the apartment, and I want to be able to hear what goes on."

"Reed, I will not tape-record what he says.

I can't tell you why, but that appalls me. To tape-record someone's conversation when he hasn't been warned is as paradigmatic of what's wrong with the world today as anything I can think of."

"Granted. So you'd rather let him get away with Winifred's murder, or succeed in silencing you with no one the wiser."

"Ends and means, Reed, it's always ends justifying means. That's how it all gets started. Our motives are pure, so it's all right if we do what the bullies and tyrants do."

"All right, we won't record it. We'll compromise. We'll just fix it so that I can hear the conversation. That way, I can call in the troops, if necessary, or come to your aid; I can also testify to what he said, though I can hardly wait for the moment in court when I'm asked in cross-examination why I didn't record the conversation, and I answer, 'Because my wife considers tape recorders immoral.' Never mind, I'll go along with you if you'll go along with me. After all, if I'd wanted to spend my life with a sensible woman, I'd have married much earlier, and not you. But you must agree to meet him here, and to traduce your Girl Scout soul far enough to lie about your being alone here. Take heart, he may not ask; he may just assume it."

Kate was silent with her eyes shut for so long that Reed wondered if she'd fallen asleep. Then she opened them. "You're on," was all she said.

Getting Martin Heffenreffer to the apartment turned out to be easier than Kate could even have hoped, let alone anticipated. He was glad enough to see her when she called expressing an interest in his work; indeed, so pleased that she concluded he had not seen the ad and was very lonely. It was child's play to arrange the meeting for her apartment. That he might misinterpret the invitation as a more personal one than Kate intended was always a danger, but all things considered, hardly a major one. Only the Stan Wymans of the world assumed that every woman was dying for their sexual attentions, which perhaps explained the paucity of their successes, if Leighton's analysis was to be believed. Reed had no difficulty setting up the eavesdropping system while Kate was out of the room; no point in rubbing it in. He also saw no point in mentioning that there would be a policeman in the room with him, someone with a gun and the ability to forget what he had heard, if necessary, and who owed Reed a favor.

Kate had invited Martin for tea or a drink,

Reed having persuaded her that the earlier the meeting started, the better. Martin, given his choice on the phone, had, unlike Richard Fothingale, chosen beer.

From the moment he arrived and sat on the edge of a chair, his arms resting on his knees, it was clear that Martin was nervous and exhausted. Well, Kate reminded himself, he's lost his love and his wife, and a large stake in his children. He needn't be a murderer to look harried.

Kate was able to open the conversation naturally enough by speaking of her recent interest in Charlotte Stanton, without, of course, mentioning what had led her to that interest. Martin seemed ready enough to speak of her, despite the fact that he must have known of Stanton's connection with Winifred. But Kate had mentioned reading the papers from the Houston MLA session, and there was no reason to suspect her motives.

"Stanton's always being compared to Graves," Martin said, "and I think that's unfortunate. They've nothing in common but a classical education and a gift for storytelling. Graves was a poet, and full of mystical ideas about the White Goddess and other fancy theories. Stanton was a very down-to-earth person, from all I can gather. They're compared also because they were both at Oxford at the same time, but all that says really is that they're almost the same generation. I don't think there's much to discuss about their similarities beyond that."

"Do you like Stanton's novels?" Kate asked, really curious.

"They're okay. She's more of a romantic than Graves; she portrays individuals — fictional, of course — with higher motives, a greater sense of honor and personal integrity than does Graves. He's likelier to see the sinister motives in those in power. And there's another odd thing. He wrote of women — have you read *Homer's Daughter*, or even the Claudius novels? Stanton seemed to scorn women. I've noticed that women consider it unrealistic to put women into stories set in ancient Greece, but men don't, at least some men don't. What do you make of that?"

Kate found herself interested by his conversation, and attracted by his observations. Well, was that so surprising? Not all murderers are brutes, obviously; perhaps only those who get found out. Intelligence must count for something, here as elsewhere. "I've noticed it often," she answered. "As though scholarly women are afraid of being accused of being fanciful, whereas men can take the chance. And Graves wasn't holding down an academic position; remember that."

"You mean, it was all right for her to write popular novels about ancient Greeks, as long as she maintained a high standard of syntax and didn't make too much up for which she hadn't evidence?"

Kate nodded. She was quiet for a time, offering him another drink, deciding to take the plunge, when he took it for her.

"I used to know someone who knew Charlotte Stanton when she was a child," he astonishingly said. "Since you seemed to be looking for her in that ad of yours, I assumed you knew her too."

"I didn't know her, I'm sorry to say," Kate said, handing him his beer. "In fact, I put that ad in because I wondered where she'd got to."

"What made you wonder?" he asked.

"A friend of mine was looking for her and couldn't find her," Kate said. Near enough to the truth. In fact, the truth.

Martin merely nodded, and drank. Kate, although she had meant to put him out of her mind, thought of Reed listening and wondered what he was making of this. What was she to do? Come out with it: Where did you put her body? How did you kill her?

"I've met your wife," Kate said. "I've seen

your house. I ought not to have asked you here without telling you that; so now you know."

"So it was Winifred you wanted to talk about. I guess I always knew. I guess what I couldn't resist was the thought of talking about her. I loved her, you know; I'll always love her."

"Do you ever think of her in your basement?" Kate not so much said as heard herself say. My God, she thought — invoking, as was a common enough habit, a being in whom she did not believe — what have I done?

"My basement?" Martin repeated, as though Kate had said "the moon." "What do you mean, my basement?"

So they had been wrong about that. No, he was lying. He had always planned to lie. I am lousy at this job, Kate thought.

"All right," she said, suddenly angry, "let's just make it a question: What did you do with her body?"

"What body?"

"Winifred's," Kate all but shouted. "Isn't that who we're talking about? Isn't that who's disappeared?"

"Jesus Christ," Martin said. "You think I killed her. You think I killed Winifred. Well, why not, why shouldn't you think that? I don't know how much you know about all this, but you're not far wrong. I wanted to kill her, at least, I discovered I wanted to kill her. I'm obsessed by her, but I'm trying to get over it. I'm not doing very well, but I didn't kill her. Thank God, I didn't kill her."

"Tell me about it," was all Kate could say.

"Starting when? When I met her? Do you know how we met? It was through Charlotte Stanton, in fact. But perhaps you knew that."

"I didn't know, but I guessed," Kate said. "Don't start with when you met her. Start with your meeting with her at Kennedy airport, when Stan Wyman saw you."

"Oh God, yes, Stan Wyman. He always had the hots for Biddy."

"Why was Winifred there? Why did she come back so suddenly from England? Start there," Kate said.

Martin got up and began pacing the room. His body was taut, like a tennis player's before serving, and for the first time Kate realized the possible danger from a man at the edge of violence and likely to pass over the edge at the merest touch. "You can't imagine the state I was in," he said, and Kate thought: You're giving me a pretty good idea. Kate had known few men who became physically wrought up in this way, who shook their fists and moved about frantically. Suddenly he stopped, stared out of the window, his back to Kate, and spoke.

"When I came upon Biddy and Winifred, laughing together — the sort of laughter only long affection can account for — I thought I would go mad, quite literally mad. Later, I accosted Winifred. It was her I minded about, you know, not Biddy — of course, I minded them knowing each other so well, but it was Winifred I felt betrayed by: she'd gone behind my back to my wife; she was a spy in the enemy country; there isn't a horrible metaphor I didn't employ. I tell you, I was close to madness. I confronted Winifred . . . oh, not long after, when I thought I had enough control of myself not to kill her, not, at any rate, to beat her up — I did hit her, you know, I hit her so hard she nearly fell, which frightened me. She said it had been an accident, they had met by accident, but that didn't console me, not much it didn't. 'Okay,' I said, 'but when you found out Biddy was my wife, when you heard her name was Heffenreffer — it's not that common a name after all — you should have just faded, you should have given a false name and said "nice to have met you" and disappeared. God knows you've had lots of practice at disappearing. You're hardly the world's expert on keeping in touch.

Why was it necessary to go on seeing her?' "
Martin was lost in the story now, Kate forgotten. How long he must have needed to tell it to someone, how often he must have told it to himself.

"She simply left me, of course; she took a job on some damn farm. I didn't know where she was; neither did anyone. I tell you, I nearly went crazy with anger. Don't ask me why; I don't know, though I've tried to think about it. I wanted her to myself, you see. I loved her like I'd never loved anyone — not even Biddy, not even the children. It was an obsession, I guess, but a quiet one. I mean, till I found out about her and Biddy, I didn't know I was obsessed. I just thought I was happy. I thought: Life is wonderful as they said it could be. Don't ask me who 'they' is. I guess I must have known it was a precarious situation: Biddy was bound to find out one day, somehow or other; wives always do. The truth is, I used to picture myself discussing it with her, after she found out, I calm, reasonable, apologetic but firm, she pleading. I ought to be ashamed to say it, but that's how I pictured it. And then I learned that they'd known all about it; that I was useful to both of them. That Winifred loved me, but loved Biddy too; Biddy loved me, but loved Winifred. Can you imagine what that was like?"

He seemed to have become aware of a listener, and faced her with the question, but it was rhetorical. He assumed no listener could imagine what it was like.

"Winifred took off, and Biddy and I tried to patch things up. What a joke. Every time I looked at her, I felt betrayed, as though she'd had an affair with my best friend. The kids were all that kept me at all sane, and even so they weren't happy. They sensed — shit, they *heard* — the problem. I used to shout, and Biddy shouted too, after a while. Who's to blame her? I hated her so for finding Winifred, for loving Winifred, for being Winifred's friend. I couldn't forgive her that, ever. It was pretty clear we better split up, Biddy and I, for the sake of the kids, as I guess they always say, don't they?

"In the end, Biddy kept the house; I couldn't have stood it anyway, and I did have to think of the kids. I have them on weekends and vacations, and those times aren't too bad. They wanted to have fun, to be with me, and I acted like every divorced father; I became the guy you had special times with, good times. I've heard divorced men say they saw far more of their children after the divorce than before, but I'd been a full-time father; Biddy and I shared it all. But I was glad of the chance not to have to impose schedules, and discipline, because I didn't trust myself to be anything but indulgent. I was afraid of my anger, even the least bit of anger.

"But the anger kept growing. People use the word *obsession*, but they don't know what they're saying. I've now read about obsessive types and that's me. There was nothing in my head but Winifred. Oh, life went on. Obsessive people can appear to be functioning just fine; that's why they get away with it for so long, and everyone's surprised as hell when they burst forth into some insane act. What it ended up with was — I had to find her, I simply had to. It wasn't all that hard, either. I got out of Biddy the postcard she'd had from Winifred — I terrified her into giving it to me, did she tell you that? Probably she didn't. Wonderful, decent Biddy. People don't expect a woman that stacked to be that decent, but that's just another of the fool ideas we all live with. I went to the post office I got off the postmark on the card, and I asked where I could find her. It was that simple. But in the end, I didn't see her. I still had that much control. I was afraid — I'm not sure of what: that I'd kill her, that I'd make such a scene she or someone would call the police. Anyway, at least I could think of her where she was."

He stopped talking for a moment, and gulped his beer. Kate refilled his glass, but he didn't notice her; he was away, he was back in his story.

"I tried to keep away from that farm, but in the end I knew I had to see her. I went back there. I hovered. No one ever saw me, you know. I'd become a sneak, a con man. I couldn't see her anywhere. That didn't mean that much; but then the farmer came out to do the milking — I was there damn early in the morning. I don't suppose you know about obsessions. It was Winifred's job to do the milking, I'd figured that out. I crept around to her A-frame, but I couldn't see in; there didn't seem to be anyone there. And then I saw the mailman arrive and put mail into the farmer's box. He was still in the barn. There was no one in sight, so I grabbed the mail out of the box, one of those rural-delivery-type mailboxes. The mailman hadn't even shut the box tight; it didn't make any noise when I opened it. There was a card from Winifred with a picture of the hotel where she was staying. She must have picked it up in the hotel lobby. It just said she was staying there, but liked her A-frame better. London was great. She'd be back in a few days. I read it, and it took all the strength I possessed to put that card back. I'd have given my life for that card, if it had been addressed to me.

"Then I went crazy again. Finally, I called her at that hotel in London. I kept trying till I got her. I told her unless she flew back on the next plane, I'd kill Biddy and the children. The way I sounded, I don't doubt she believed me. She was right to believe me; I was mad. She said she would take the next plane back. She did. Winifred always kept her word. I just hung around the airport from the first possible moment she could have arrived. I met every plane from London. I'd told her I'd meet her at Kennedy; I said I'd be waiting. And I waited."

For the first time since Martin had begun talking, Kate thought of Reed, hearing all this. What would he make of it? What was she making of it? I've never heard a confession before, she thought. I've never understood why confessions are so convincing; why we believe them, why priests believe them, and why they seem so real on videotape, as Reed says they do a good part of the time. We go through life, and there's so little we know. Martin, who had paused for another gulp, another stare out the window, spoke again.

"I'd made a reservation at a hotel in the air-

309

port. When she came through into the baggage area, I saw her as though she had a spotlight on her. I think I could find her in a crowd of thousands, I could spot her anywhere. She didn't have any baggage checked through, she said, only the shoulder bag she had with her. I took her off to the room. When I saw her there, when I took her in my arms, I started to weep — bawl, I mean — as though I'd never stop. She held me. She didn't say much. I don't know what she understood. I didn't tell her all this, I didn't tell her much of anything. I made love to her — my God, it didn't even occur to me to ask her if she was hungry. I didn't ask her anything. I clung to her as though we were on a sea, and she was all there was in sight that floated. Then I fell asleep, into the first sound sleep I'd had since the day I saw them both there, laughing in that goddamn restaurant. I don't know how long I slept, but I woke up because she was shouting 'Martin, Martin' and pulling at my arms. And I was on top of her, choking her; I was trying to kill her, and I was asleep. Can you picture that? I was killing her in my sleep.

"Something broke inside me then. I knew that if I didn't take desperate measures — what are the words that don't sound cheap, that haven't been overused in a hundred stupid films and books? — someone would be killed. I was out of control. So you pictured me burying Winifred in the basement. Well, you weren't far wrong. I'd have buried someone, or killed myself.

"Winifred understood that. 'What can I do, Martin?' she said. 'Just tell me what I can do.' And I said: 'Go away, far away, as far as a plane can take you. And stay there; don't ever come back. Promise me you'll never come back.' 'If I go,' she said, 'how will I know Biddy will be all right, and the children?' I told her it was a bargain. I promised her, and I meant it. If I knew she was out of reach, out of everyone's reach in my world, not in any country where Biddy could get to her, or run into her, not even in the hemisphere, I could manage. I could promise her Biddy and the kids would be all right. 'Where shall I go?' she said, just like that. I told her I didn't mean right that minute, I meant in a while. 'No,' she said, 'let's arrange it now. But how will I pay for the ticket?' I told her I'd put it on my American Express card. I'd found out when Biddy went to California that you could pay for travel over five or six months. I'd manage that. So we just walked out of the hotel room. She had her flight bag on her shoulder. She spent some time in the bathroom, and that was the only preparation she made, for going around the world. We went to Pan Am, which seemed a likely airline, and there was a flight to India leaving in a few hours. We bought her a ticket. She had her passport. It must sound insane, told this way, but that's how it happened. 'I'm used to traveling light, and to impulsive moves, Martin; don't worry about me. I've always wanted to see what it's like in other parts of the world. I may not stay in India. I may go who knows where. But I won't return to America or Europe — not, at least, for as long as I can see ahead. All right, Martin? Will you try to get over this obsession? Try anything there is: religion, psychoanalysis, whatever will help. Will you do that in your turn?' "

Martin was calmer now. He turned from pacing, turned from the window, and sat down opposite Kate. He poured himself more beer. "She actually left," he said. "We had a meal in the airport restaurant; that's where Stan Wyman saw us. She held out her hand when he held out his and said, 'I'm Winifred Ashby.' He must have seen I was besotted with her. Even that fool could see that much. He didn't hang around, thank God. Winifred wrote a letter to the people who paid out her

312

little income, telling them to send her checks to the American Express office in Delhi. I mailed it later. What she felt worst about was the farmers. She had given them her word she would return. I pointed out that as far as anyone knew, she would have disappeared, so they wouldn't think she'd deserted only them. I think that comforted her somewhat. When she got on the plane, I knew that I'd been saved from some terrible fate — that we all had. Crazy? Sure it's crazy. So are many things we never know about as we live our tidy lives. I used to say I was obsessed with Biddy when we first met and I wanted to marry her. But I didn't know what obsession is. No one knows who hasn't been there." He fell silent. It seemed to Kate his voice had been filling the room for hours, for longer than she could count. They just sat there, feeling the silence. Then Martin spoke, differently:

"I don't know where she is," he said, "but I know she's alive. I know because I can feel it; if she were not alive, I'd feel it. That may not make a great deal of sense; believe it or not. She's alive, but I don't know where she is. I'll never know."

"Another beer?" Kate asked, after a time. "Would you like anything else?" What was there to say, except to play the hostess, to offer nourishment of the only kind available.

"I'll be going," Martin said. "You've done me good. I'm glad you know what happened. I have to trust you not to talk. Will you tell anyone?"

"I'll have to," Kate said. "That is, I'll have to tell a number of people that Winifred went to India, and that we don't know where she is; that she doesn't expect to return. I won't tell anyone except my husband what you've told me, unless I have to. I can't think why I would have to, but you never know."

"I'll settle for that," Martin said. "I'm trying a number of distractions. I think I'll be all right. All right for the children, and my students, I mean. I'll never be really all right for anything again. We began," he said, standing in the hallway, "by talking about Graves and Stanton. I'll tell you one difference between them. I think Graves would have understood this obsession. Stanton wouldn't have."

"I think you're wrong," Kate said. "Goodbye." And she held out her hand. Martin took it. What right had he to do what he'd done? Kate thought. Why did I shake his hand? Because, she thought, he had won his struggle, and Winifred was a wanderer at heart. He had not exiled her. Whatever she was in search of,

Winifred could not be exiled. She belonged to no place special. I need a drink, Kate thought. A double martini. Where the hell is Reed?

Seventeen

Reed, having let the plainsclothesman out the door, came into the living room and held Kate in his arms. She was shaking; he held her until she became still and moved from him to pour herself a long glass of club soda, which she drank thirstily. "Who was that man?" she asked.

"He was an old friend from the police, my unofficial companion in eavesdropping. No, don't worry," he said, reaching out for her as she began to protest. "He'll forget everything he heard tonight unless, for some unforeseen reason, we ask him to remember it. I admit he was unnecessary, as it turned out, but do try to remember, dear Kate, that you were in here alone with a man capable of murder, and one whom I thought had already committed murder. As you may have noticed, I am not your James Bond type."

"I did promise not to tell anyone. . . ."

"And you haven't; nor will the policeman. You're not really worried about the policeman."

"Reed, I feel two powerful and contradictory emotions at the same time, and I can't seem to get them to settle down together in my mind."

"That she's alive, and that she's lost."

"Lost to all of us, yes. Didn't you find it strange, her agreeing to go like that, at once, so far?"

"No," Reed said, "and neither will you when the shock of all this is past. I think his demand answered some need in her; she's a seeker, she's looking for something." Kate cocked an eyebrow at him.

"No," Reed said, "I don't mean something profound or mystical; she's not looking for an answer; she's far too intelligent — too wise, if you don't mind the word — to think there is one. I'm sure she isn't after 'peace of mind' or anything like that. But I think she wants to experience something beyond what seems to be available in our 'developed,' if that's the word, civilization. Look at it practically: she's a vigorous woman; she can fix machinery and care for farm animals. She has a gift for friendship and for solitude, an excellent combination. A lot of people, I've noticed, like to think they have a gift for solitude, but they don't. Either they're not alone as much as they imagine or they're just plain lonely. Winifred will be all right. She may even be happy. Maybe she fell in with his demands, but I don't think she would have done that just to assuage him. It wouldn't have made sense, and Winifred makes sense."

"You're right," Kate said. "I see that. I'm just being childish. Once I knew she wasn't dead, I wanted her produced on the spot, or at least promised for a few days hence. Charlie will feel the same. I'll have to tell them, Charlie and Toby and Leighton, and I guess Biddy too, that Winifred's gone, but alive. So that's over."

"What you need," Reed said, "is something to eat. Not hungry? How about a drink. This is the sort of situation where you require brandy forced down your throat. It's a shock, my love, and you can't expect to recover in minutes. Here, drink this, and just let me hold you."

Kate leaned against him on the couch. "What will happen to the money to come to her from Sinjin's will? How will she get it? She'll need it, won't she?"

"Either she'll let someone know where to send it or it will accumulate until called for. She'll know it's waiting, should she need it. That's the best function of money anyway. I'm glad you're asking questions. That shows you're recovering. I was scared there for a minute."

Toby, Charlie, and Biddy took the news much as Kate had — relieved and, not quite simultaneously, disappointed. They asked endless questions, naturally enough, and Kate did her best to respond without answering them. There wasn't that much to explain, since Martin had to be kept out of the account of Winifred's sudden decision to go far away. But, as Reed had understood, that decision did not seem uncharacteristic to anyone who had known Winifred, or even heard about her, so Kate's task was easier than it might have been.

Leighton, unlike the others, was silent when she heard the news, and hung up after a few minutes of perfunctory conversation following Kate's report. A few days later, she called, asking to have "brunch" with Kate — it was a Sunday, and that was the meal served in New York restaurants in the middle of Sunday.

"But I don't want to go to a fancy joint," Leighton said. "I know a place with booths where you can get bacon and eggs and real home-fried potatoes, not a prepared imitation. Will you meet me there?" And Kate said she would, remarking, however, to Reed as she left the house that she had a scary feeling about what Leighton was going to say.

"I know," Reed said, "in your bones. Your bones were wrong about Winifred, who isn't dead."

"I hope they're wrong about this too," Kate said, "but I could hear trouble in every syllable she uttered on the phone. As an aunt, one is supposed to have only frivolous pleasures with the young of the family."

"Nonsense," Reed told her. "You don't believe that for a minute. I like Leighton. No real problem with her. You'll see."

Leighton was already there, in a booth, when Kate arrived at the coffee shop, as it called itself, which resembled diners as they were when Kate was young and her family could never be persuaded to eat in them. As a result, she adored them, and told Leighton so, sliding onto the bench across from Leighton. "I'm even prepared to eat according to your suggestion, which seems to encompass all that is today considered most lethal. If we

320

can manage to pour salt all over everything, we should hit the forbidden diet jackpot." Leighton gave their order to the waitress. "Anything to drink?" the waitress asked. They ordered coffee, *with* caffeine. "And cream," Kate added with the air of one about to be hung for a sheep.

"I don't really think the role of Watson suited me," Leighton said.

"Of course it didn't. You want to tell your own story, not be a recording machine."

"Kate," Leighton said, in the tone of one preparing an invalid for the idea of a necessary operation.

"Yes, Leighton, what is it? Tell me fast, so that I can digest this marvelously unhealthy lunch."

"I'm going to India. I'm going to look for Winifred."

Kate stared. Whatever possibilities had been skimming across her mind, this was not among them. "She may not even have stayed in India, Leighton. Anyway, India is an enormous country. And what will you do there?"

"The plane will stop in London, and I'll get off and see if I can find out who's paying out her income, and where they're sending it. Charlie might have an idea. But if that doesn't work, I'll just go to New Delhi and begin there."

"Are you sure it isn't just that you want something to do, any quest, the result of being in a loose-endish time?"

"There is that danger," Leighton said, as the waitress put down their plates. "I see that. But I don't really think that's it. I want to find Winifred — in the flesh, I mean — and I want to see another part of the world. Don't worry, Kate; I'll manage."

Kate began to eat. It was delicious. Like mashed potatoes and gravy, she thought, something we've sacrificed to health foods and gourmet cooking. She found it hard to say what she was feeling. "Leighton, can I be frank?"

"Can a porcupine be prickly?"

"I'm worried about gurus."

Leighton stared at her. "That may be frank, Kate, but it's not exactly comprehensible."

"I'm worred you are, or might be, one of those Americans looking for a faith, looking for a master, a guru, looking for a religion, a way to higher thought — damn it, Leighton, you know perfectly well what I mean."

"I do now. Kate, you'll have to believe me. I mean, I can't convince you if you won't believe me, or think I don't know myself, or anything like that. I don't want a faith, or a purpose in life; God knows (a joke) I don't want a master, or a priest. I can't tell you what I do want, because I'm not seeking something wonderful, or mysterious. I just want to find Winifred."

"And suppose you find her. What then?"

"Who knows? Probably she'll say: 'Nice to have met you, I'm off to Africa — or China or Arabia — and I'm going alone.' I'm not dreaming she'll say: 'So you've come. There is something we must do together.' " Leighton said this so portentously that Kate had to laugh. "I'm not lost in a fantasy, or a search for the answer to life. I just think finding Winifred is what I want to do. And when I've found her — *if* I find her — who knows? Probably I'll write a book called *In Search of Winifred*. I think it will have distinct possibilities, don't you?"

Kate sighed. What was there to say? She made a sandwich of her remaining bacon and toast, and ate it with pleasure. She felt good, she realized; living in the moment, in this sensation, and not looking over the edge into the next requirement of life. Had Leighton come to feel that too? One could either worry about Leighton or trust her, and Kate realized she had decided upon trust.

"So that's settled, then," Kate said at last, when their food was gone and they were drinking their coffee. "I'm glad you told me. Have you everything you need?"

"Not exactly," Leighton said, holding her cup in both hands. "Could I put the ticket to India on your American Express card?"

Some weeks later, Charlie had a postcard from India. It was an ordinary Indian scene, a tourist's postcard, and study it as she might, Charlie could find no significance in it. Nor was there a message. But where a message could have been, at the very bottom was a signature: "Winifred."

Charlie brought it over for Kate to see. "It's like her," Kate said. "No wasted words." Kate could say more later to Reed, when telling him about it. "She more or less promised not to be in touch; to disappear. The only one she could honorably send some sign of life to was Charlie. Martin has no connection with Charlie. And, after all, it was Charlie she had deserted in England, when she flew home to Martin. The true Winifred touch. And it reassures me, about Leighton, about everything."

It was shortly after that that Charlie and

Toby married, and were duly celebrated at the office of Dar and Dar, and at a gala dinner with Reed and Kate.

As the summer wore on, Toby was not surprised to be consulted by Larry about his annual fall party for the associates. But Larry was not worried this time; he was complacent.

"I can't think why I got the wind up about inviting my sister, about her coming to the party, I mean. Her being there didn't make the slightest difference, did it? It was good to see her, in a way. We had a nice chat. I hope she comes again. A man ought to see his kid sister once in a while, don't you think, Toby?"

All the way home Toby tried to decide if Larry had been serious. Was he capable of irony? As he entered his apartment building, Toby decided, no, no irony; Larry had been serious. Kate wouldn't come this year, of course. Toby would miss her. But, he thought, putting his key in the door and, as it opened, calling out that he was home, he would have Charlie next to him.

THORNDIKE PRESS HOPES you have enjoyed this Large Print book. All our Large Print titles are designed for the easiest reading, and all our books are made to last. Other Thorndike Press Large Print books are available at your library, through selected bookstores, or directly from the publisher. For more information about current and upcoming titles, please call us, toll free, at 1-800-223-6121, or mail your name and address to:

THORNDIKE PRESS
ONE MILE ROAD
P. O. BOX 159
THORNDIKE, MAINE 04986

There is no obligation, of course.